Running With the Devil

Book 1—the Running series

Running With the Devil*
Lorelei James
Published by LJLA, LLC
Copyright 2014, LJLA LLC
Cover Design by: Meredith Blair, *www.AuthorsAngels.com*
ISBN: 978-0-9888235-5-6

*re-release, previously published in 2007

Thanks to the thousands of men and women who descend on the little town of Sturgis, South Dakota every year in August. The wild, raunchy public exploits during the annual Sturgis Rally and Races are always an inspiration.

CHAPTER ONE

Assless chaps were all the rage in Sturgis.

Drake March sauntered through the Broken Arrow Campground, taking in the sights and sounds of the world's largest biker party.

Through the dusty haze kicked up by thousands of motorcycles, the variety of bare butts tortured him. Skin tones ranging from milk-light to coffee-dark. Flaunted breasts played peek-a-boo beneath strands of metallic-colored plastic beads. Guys snapped photos of half-naked chicks as proof they'd actually seen some titty action at the Legendary Arrow.

Vegas had nothing on the anything goes atmosphere. Blowjobs in broad daylight. Couples coupling next to the main performance stage while a Christian biker club sang about sin and redemption. A magnificent woman slinked by wearing a studded dog collar—her jeweled nipple rings were attached to a long, thin silver chain that disappeared into the crotch of her purple thong. Two topless babes were making out on a bucking mechanical bull while the drunken crowd egged them on.

No wonder his concentration was lousy.

He'd spotted another flawless ass bent over an electric blue Outlaw custom chopper when a sharp command echoed in his earpiece.

"Target spotted. Ten yards to your left. Copy."

Beneath his Ray-bans, Drake's eyes narrowed on his contact, then widened. "That's her? The redhead with the big tits?" He inwardly winced. His supervisor would ream him when she listened to the surveillance tapes. But damn, it was hard not to show pure male adoration at the way the woman filled out the miniscule black halter-top.

Ms. 40C leaned against the plywood wall of the beer garden, plastic cup in hand, a walking ad for juicy wet sex.

"I thought Jerry's files said she was blonde?"

"Guess Miss Clairol got to her before we did," Geo drawled.

"You sure it's her, Bobby?" Drake asked.

"Yep," Bobby said. "She's wearing the flag."

Drake's gaze zoomed over the white ribbon tied on her left arm and down, past the golden bell winking in her navel. A skintight leopard print miniskirt molded curvy hips. The ensemble ended with a pair of glossy black thigh-high boots showcasing world-class legs on par with her world-class breasts.

He nearly stumbled over his tongue. *Jerry my man, you had exquisite taste.*

"Drake, you there?"

"Roger that, I'm on it."

"You mean on her, you lucky son-of-a-bitch," Geo groused in his ear. "Next time, I get to be point man and you get to coordinate recon in the damn truck."

"You wish. Stay alert, Bobby. I'm switching to B-mode." Bobby was his ground support. Drake removed the lip mic, leaving the small earpiece intact. For all intents and purposes he resembled just another security goon.

Raking a hand though his hair, he started toward the mysterious woman, remembering at the last second to paste on a smile.

Her demeanor didn't change at his approach, save for the imperceptible tightening of her blood-red mouth. Dark maroon sunglasses rested on an aquiline nose, hiding her eyes. But he sensed beneath those cheap shades she studied him intently.

"Kenna?"

"Yes?"

"Jerry Travis asked me to meet you here."

Her assessing gaze started at his Caterpillar boots and traveled up every inch of his six-foot-four-inch frame. She tilted her head back and murmured, "Seems old Jerry's come up in the world."

"Can we go someplace private to talk?"

She lifted the cup to her mouth, running the tip of her pink tongue along the rim before tossing the empty container into the garbage can. "Maybe. If I've got the right incentive."

He grinned. "Name your price."

"Sugar, you couldn't afford me." She untied the ribbon from her arm, zigzagging it up his forearm, soft as a whisper. After she'd wrapped it around his bicep, her fingers smoothed the satiny strap, lingering on his muscle flexing beneath it. "But I'll admit you've piqued my interest."

Drake suppressed a shudder of raw pleasure. A whiskey-warmed voice and cool caress on his heated skin; this woman packed a powerful punch. The kind of visceral reaction he hadn't allowed himself to feel in ages.

"There's an empty table about fifty feet to your left. I'll join you there in a minute."

"Where you gonna be?"

"Getting a beer. Want one?"

A barrel-chested man stopped and gave Kenna a once over followed by a sharp wolf whistle. "I'll buy you the whole damn keg or whatever else turns your crank, honey, if you'll ride around on the back of my hog today."

Her sultry siren act vanished. "No thanks."

His beefy, hairy shoulders lifted. "Your loss."

She shuffled her feet, a sign she might bolt.

Screw that. Drake had waited too damn long for this. "Maybe you should come along as I grab that beer."

"Maybe you should hurry the hell up before I get bored with this cryptic conversation and disappear." She spun on her stiletto boots, ass swaying beneath her body-hugging skirt, wild red hair brushing her shoulders.

Great. He'd hoped not to spook her, but thanks to that lowlife biker she was wound tight as a whore in church. He paid for the draft and picked his way through the trash littering the flattened grass and sinkholes to the rickety picnic table.

He'd barely slid onto the bench seat when she demanded, "Cut the shit. Who are you?"

Wow. She'd changed from simpering to seething pretty damn quick. "Name's Drake," he said, sipping his ice-cold beer.

"What do you want?"

"To talk to you."

"So you said. Where is Jerry?"

He gazed at her over the top of his sunglasses. God she was striking, not the washed-up druggie he'd expected. He floated a deliberate pause, announced, "Dead," and waited for her response.

No sound escaped those ruby lips, but she arched back as if making a move to leave.

Without missing a beat, Drake wrapped his big hand around her smaller wrist and yanked her closer until those bountiful breasts were within licking distance. He smiled—all teeth.

"Let go, you fucking psycho."

"Now Kenna. Is that any way to talk?"

"How about: If you don't let go of me right fucking now I'll break your fucking nose. Is that more fucking polite?"

Her tone was so chillingly matter-of-fact he suspected she probably could. Or was it a con? And why the hell did the tough chick act make his dick hard?

Drake grinned, slow and easy. "If I do let go, promise you won't make me chase you down? Because I have no qualms about tackling your sweet ass right into the dirt, sweetheart."

"Bet you'd like that."

"You have no idea." He loosened his death-grip in a show of faith. "All I want is to talk to you. Then you're free to go." *Unless you'll somehow prove useful to me and then you couldn't pry me from your side with a crowbar.*

She seemed to consider it before she nodded.

"Good." He released her wrist and she rubbed the spot he'd touched like he'd somehow marked her soft skin.

And her attitude got to him. Oh, he would like to mark her. Eat at that abundant mouth until it was swollen from his hard kisses. Trail his teeth across the slender column of her neck and lower to bestow slow, thorough love bites around each nipple. He'd suck a path down her smooth belly. Flick his wet tongue over that intriguing little bell in her navel. Settle his mouth on her engorged sex until she writhed and bucked beneath his punishing lips, sharp teeth and lashing tongue.

"Get on with the damn questions then."

Whoa. Talk about reverting to juvenile fantasies. He kept his face impassive even when his body protested the sudden shift from boiling point to deep freeze. "When was the last time you heard from Jerry?"

"He emailed me two days ago, asking that I meet him here instead of our normal place. Didn't tell me why."

Drake removed his sunglasses hoping it'd prompt her to do the same. "Do you always do what Jerry asks?"

She tapped her fingers on the table next to an enormous purse beaded in a rainbow pattern. "Only when I get email from a dead man. Then I get very curious."

That floored him. "You knew Jerry was dead?"

"Yep." She paused, showed her pearly whites. "I assume *you* sent that bogus email?"

His answering smile was equally tight.

She ripped off her shades and his breath snagged in his throat. Jesus. Not only were her eyes snapping fire, they were the most unusual shade of blue he'd ever seen. Almost purple.

"Why—"

"Why did you show up here anyway if you knew the email was a fake?" He watched her delicate nostrils flare outrage. Why his cock took particular delight in her show of feminine temper was a mystery.

"To see what kind of freak uses a dead friend as a way to hook up with chicks. What the fuck is wrong with you? Suggesting I tie a ribbon around my goddamn arm like some kind of primitive cowbell?" She actually growled annoyance. "I came here to kick your balls up your ass. I don't know what Jerry told you and I don't give a flying fuck if you've got some weird James Bond fetish—"

"Whoa whoa whoa. Hang on a sec. Jerry didn't tell me anything. That's why I had to use his email address to get a message to you."

Confusion pulled her lush mouth into a flat line.

"Would you have shown up otherwise?"

She shook her head.

"Kenna, you're one of his last known contacts."

"And you're just getting around to talking to me *now?*"

Drake sighed. "Look. I'd been working with Jerry for the last few months. He disappeared. His body was found two weeks ago."

"I know. What does that have to do with me?"

"Yours was the only file I found when I hacked into his computer. He had it hidden in a subdirectory." He paused. "Fascinating reading. I can see why he kept it."

Her body stayed still. Only the twitch beneath her left eye gave away her unease. "You think I had something to do with his death?"

"It's possible. Seems he paid you ten grand last year. Why?" He sipped his beer, locking his gaze with hers. "Were you black-mailing him?"

She smirked and lifted her shoulder in a half-shrug.

"He funding your drug habit?"

The smug smile died. "Piss off."

"Ah. So you are a pro."

A shadow fell across her face. Drake glanced up, glaring at the heavy-set couple in matching Bermuda shorts and Wall Drug T-shirts. They backed off and found another picnic table to eat their Indian tacos.

He refocused on Kenna, letting his inner slimeball surface. He'd get to the bottom of her connection to Jerry Travis no matter how distasteful he found this balls-to-the-wall type of questioning. Especially with a woman who'd piqued far more of his personal curiosity than was wise. "You must be a wildcat between the sheets to earn that kind of cash."

"Fuck you. I don't need this shit and I don't have to answer any more of your asinine questions."

Again his hand snaked out and encircled her wrist. "I'm afraid you do have to answer my questions, Ms. Jones." He smiled but knew it didn't reach his eyes. "Guess I neglected to fully introduce myself. Agent Drake March. DEA."

Fuck. It figured.

First time she'd ever felt an immediate inexplicable attraction and the jerk turned out to be another phony.

Hey, at least she was consistent.

Kenna tugged hard at his enormous hand, knowing those meat hooks could easily bruise her skin. Crossing her arms on the table, she waited for him to explain himself or flash his badge, but he seemed absorbed with figuring out her bra cup size.

He looked up. "For the record, let's start over."

No kidding she'd like to start the whole day over. Minus the trip to the Broken Arrow. Minus a run-in with a DEA agent.

As a grad student working on federal land, she'd dealt with the FBI, the tribal police and the jerks from OSHA. Even other agencies steered clear of the DEA, as they did whatever the hell they wanted and reveled in their "lone wolf" approach to law enforcement.

She stared at him, wondering when her cop radar had jammed. True, the man didn't look like a Fed, with his unruly mane of black hair, unshaven jaw and I'd-like-to-ride-you-hard-for-hours hungry stare. Add in the faded gray T-shirt stretched across a powerfully built chest, biceps that'd make a body builder weep, and she'd pegged him as serious muscle for somebody, just not for the damn government. But those cold, piercing blue eyes should've been a dead giveaway.

Dead. She glanced down at the mint-green paint peeling away from the metal anchors on the table, hiding her pained expression.

Hard to fathom Jerry had been brutally murdered. He might've looked the quintessential badass biker—long hair, tats, piercings and attitude—but she hadn't assumed he was a criminal.

These days it was difficult to tell the doctors, lawyers and stockbrokers from the real bikers. A brazen display of "colors" was usually the only clear sign. Since Jerry had been thoughtful and surprisingly shy, she hadn't wasted brainpower contemplating whether he'd been involved in illegal activities. So...why was the DEA interested in her?

"Kenna?"

She jumped. Not only were Agent March's good looks lethal, his sexy voice could melt bedrock. "What?"

"Tell me how you met Jerry."

Hmm. Continue the lie? Or tell the truth? "Through a friend."

One black brow winged up. "A pimp?"

"Wrong conclusion, bub. He was an old friend of my neighbor, Marissa Cruz. Our association was strictly business since Jerry came to Sturgis looking for a tour guide, not a mattress monkey."

Disbelief pulled his intriguing lips into a scowl.

She knew it sounded far-fetched and as much as she didn't want to explain, she knew she'd have to. "Remember the fat dude who offered me the moon if I'd hop on his bike?"

He nodded.

"That's nothing. It's common practice around these parts for men to shell out money, lots of money, to have me—or a woman like me—ride around on the back of their Harley during the Rally."

"How much money?"

"I got paid a thousand dollars a day."

He whistled. "What did Jerry get for a thousand bucks?"

"Me, decked out in a skimpy outfit, perched behind him on the bike. We hit the bars, rode around in the Hills, paraded down the main drag, attended private parties." She shrugged. "If a guy is willing to drop fifty to a hundred grand on a motorcycle, another couple of thousand bucks is chump change. Besides, it's the ultimate big dick contest to show off custom bikes with a scantily clad hot babe clinging to their back."

His mouth opened; she held up a hand to stop his inevitable question. "Before you ask, no, I didn't screw him. Ever."

"But don't people get suspicious if you're with biker guy 'A' on Monday and biker guy 'B' on Tuesday?"

Kenna laughed. "Are you serious? With more than half a million people milling around Sturgis? I can change my look"—she snapped her fingers—"like that." She angled forward and challenged, "Tomorrow I could be a brunette, waltz right by you on Main Street stark naked and you'd never recognize me."

Agent March's eyes descended to her cleavage, then homed in on her mouth before his steely blue gaze reconnected with hers. "There are some things you can't hide or fake, Kenna."

A punch of lust rolled through her. "Regardless. Last year Jerry wanted someone to tool around with and act like his girlfriend. I was it. End of story."

"And the other three grand he paid you in January?"

Her gaze darted to the beer garden, away from those cool knowing eyes. "A bonus," she lied.

"Why the guilty face, if you did nothing wrong?"

"Not because I slept with him, you perv." No doubt he'd be suspicious if she confessed to the "errands" she'd run for Jerry in the last year for the three thousand dollar bonus. She'd been skeptical herself about the contents of those mysterious packages. But Jerry had been sweetly insistent, reminding her that he'd helped her out of a bind, offered to pay her for her trouble, and she'd felt…well, *obligated* to him. So she'd made the drops and put it out of her mind. Until now. She swallowed the bad taste in her mouth. "What does the DEA want with him anyway? Was he a snitch?"

Again those fascinating indigo eyes locked to hers.

Her stomach gave a little flip when he looked at her in an entirely different way than she was accustomed. Granted, it took considerable effort for most men to keep their lustful gazes on her face, not her bust. But this man seemed to be trying to see her soul.

Yeah right. Mr. DEA was probably trying to figure out whether or not she was high.

"Snitch is such a juvenile word," Agent March said finally. "Jerry was an informant."

"Always?"

He shook his head, sending a hank of hair cascading over his eye, an unconsciously sexy gesture.

But she was acutely conscious of it.

Kenna's fingers curled into her palms against the desire to sweep back those silky black strands. Crush them in her hands and yank that pouty mouth to hers to answer the question foremost on *her* mind: Did he know how to use those yummy lips as expertly as she suspected?

And if the hot looks he'd been shooting her were any indication, he wouldn't do a damn thing to resist.

God. What was wrong with her? Maybe she'd fastened her wig too tight and it was cutting off blood to her brain.

Or the hedonistic atmosphere around here *was* contagious.

He drained the last of his beer. "Jerry was just another lowlife thug making runs for a Florida drug dealer. Did he mention anything to you about Diablo?"

"No. What is Diablo?"

"Unconfirmed rumor it's a group breaking away from the Miami drug cartel looking to start their own operations in the Midwest. No one knows who's running it. Except it seems Jerry inadvertently stumbled across some information during his trip to Sturgis last year. He came to us six months ago, whining Diablo played dirty."

"Honor among thieves?"

"Nothing that noble. Seems Diablo planned to intentionally sell deadly batches of bad meth, blaming it on the local distributors—who have loyalties to Jerry's boss in Miami. Diablo steps in with their cheaper product and takes over distribution of all venues." Drake's broad chest cast the picnic table in shadow when he moved forward. "You were with Jerry last year. Which means you've met with some of the key players."

"Me? I'm just arm candy, remember? I wouldn't know a drug dealer from a car dealer."

His slow, sexy smile sent her warning bells ringing. "Ah. But *I* do. And here's where I want you come in."

"And do what?"

"The same thing you did for Jerry last year. Act like my girlfriend."

"No way," she said. "I'm not getting involved."

"You already are."

Instead of panicking, she retorted, "Bite me."

"Oh I'd like to, Kenna, you know I would. And I'll even let you pick the first place I set my teeth on you."

The air between them thickened, the chipped picnic table and the raucous crowd faded away. In twenty-nine years she'd never been more aware of a man's absolute focus on her. Sexual heat radiated from him, and seeped into her pores like a warm, sensual fog. A fog intent on clouding her judgment.

She could almost sense his body crowding hers. Shivers from his hot breath teasing her skin. Hear the increased tempo of her own heartbeat as he whispered naughty suggestions in her ear. Feel the wicked touch of his hands on her breasts and stroking between her thighs. Taste his sinful mouth.

Kenna's body went taut from the phantom assault.

He reached over and toyed with a strand of hair. The back of his knuckles brushed against the arch of her neck.

Tingles burst beneath her skin, zipping through her bloodstream like tiny carbonated bubbles. Of all the moves he could have made... How did he know she craved that gentle touch, right there?

Maybe he was a sexual psychic.

Maybe she was desperate.

"Bring me to the meeting place tonight," he murmured. His husky bedroom tone fairly dripped secrets of the *Kama Sutra*.

Her nipples beaded to tender points under his shameless perusal. Throat dry, she croaked, "What are you doing?"

"Proving we won't have to act to convince people we're lovers."

Whoosh. He shattered any pretense of her indifference.

At some point during his verbal seduction, Agent March had lifted her hand to his lips. He nibbled on her fingertips. Between his lazy kisses, Kenna closed her eyes. She savored the heady sensation, completely lost in the strange way he recognized what she needed. She suspected he'd give her what she'd always craved, but been afraid to admit she even wanted.

He's a cop, her brain warned.

He's a man, her horny side argued.

He trailed hot, wet, open-mouthed kisses across the back of her hand. Darting his agile tongue between her knuckles, then just the tip of that wayward tongue in and out. "Don't go all shy on me now. Prove that sexpot routine isn't just an act, Kenna."

His warm mouth slid to the pulse point on the inside of her wrist. He flicked his tongue across the vein, keeping time with the beat of her blood.

She couldn't breathe.

His teeth scraped. Teased. He gently bit down on the fleshy part of her thumb like it was a juicy, tempting fruit.

A rush of pure pleasure exploded inside her.

Scorching summer sun, dust, the stench of sour beer, the growl of motorcycle engines intruded into her awareness as abruptly as it'd vanished.

His rough knuckles continued to lightly caress the sweat-dampened hollow of her throat.

Kenna opened her eyes, expecting to see his smug male satisfaction.

The raw hunger on his face sent her senses reeling.

Without breaking eye contact, he nuzzled her forearm and softly kissed the inside of her elbow. Then he moved her hand down his chest, placing it on his thundering heart.

The unexpectedly sweet gesture bothered her more than a smarmy comment. She jerked back.

"Too late for regrets." The sly grin she expected finally appeared. "Back to the business at hand. Where and what time should I meet you?"

She stifled a scream. Dammit. His reverent touches and lust-filled glances had been a ploy! She'd been played.

Seething, she rummaged in her purse for a diversion from his shrewd gaze. "Sorry. I'm busy."

"I thought we established you'll be busy with me."

Kenna slicked a clear coat of berry-flavored gloss over her lips, puckered and tossed the tube back inside. "You?" She laughed harshly. "Please, Agent March. You might as well tattoo your badge number on your forehead and wear a uniform. Everything about you screams *cop*."

"Fooled you, didn't I?"

"Briefly. But wearing a Harley T-shirt, jeans, boots and attaching your wallet to a dog chain won't make you a biker."

"That right?" His tone dropped an octave; the air temp plunged from the chill in his voice. "Got any more suggestions?"

"Yeah. Pull the stick out of your ass, Agent March. I'm just being honest."

Lord. He pushed her buttons. She'd spewed more cuss words in the last hour than she normally did in a year. She didn't even want to think about how one hot look from him made her want to strip them both naked and test the strength of the picnic table. In broad daylight.

She slanted forward, a little leery of the tight set to his jaw. "I'll keep my ears open and report whatever I hear back to you. Fair enough?"

"No dice. How's this for fair? You help me and I won't turn you into the Sturgis PD for solicitation."

Kenna gasped. "You wouldn't dare."

"Try me. Do you have a license for this 'escort' business you've been running?"

"It's not an escort service!"

"My point exactly." His laid-back, sexually playful attitude was a distant memory. Now his eyes were hard and cold. "A federal informant is dead. If you aren't gonna help me, then I'll make damn sure you're out of my way."

A heavy, ugly silence weighed.

He could fuck up her life with one phone call.

Kenna silently cursed her shortsightedness. When her grant had mysteriously fallen through last year at the last minute, her pal Marissa had come to the rescue. She suggested Kenna act as a highly paid tour guide for Marissa's old friend, Jerry Travis.

She'd been desperate; take the money or forfeit her place in the doctoral program. No brainer. She'd taken the cash and hadn't regretted it.

Until now.

If word got around the small academic community she'd been busted for prostitution she'd get kicked out. Wouldn't matter if it weren't true. Then it wouldn't even matter if she had the money to pay tuition.

She'd gone to a lot of trouble to make damn sure no one besides Marissa knew her alternate identity. "Kenna Jones" was completely fictional. Not even Jerry had known her real name.

Evidently Mr. DEA didn't either or he'd have contacted her at home, not by the decoy email account. At this point she owed him *nada*. She'd answered his questions. If he hadn't arrested her by now, by all rights she could get up and walk away.

Besides, it'd be interesting to see how he liked being played. The more she thought about it, the more she decided it'd serve him right. A few quick changes and she'd disappear into the throng of bikers like a nitro vapor trail.

Despite his earlier cocky statement, Agent March would be hard pressed to ever find her again.

She smiled sheepishly and said, "All right. I'm in."

Kenna was so full of shit her lavender eyeballs swam in it. The hellcat who had sworn, sneered and smoldered had gone all sweet, soft and sorry. Helpful, even.

Right. As if he'd buy that.

Yet Drake allowed her to ramble on. He nodded, appearing to swallow her heartfelt lines of apology as if they were gospel.

She'd grudgingly told him the meeting place (fat chance she'd show) and a firm time (another lie) before they said goodbye.

He admired her remarkable ass as she flitted away, an extra spring in her high-heeled step. She even stopped, turned back around, offering him a jaunty wave and a saucy grin.

Oh yeah. She was good.

But he was better.

The minute she escaped from view Drake reached into his pocket for the lip mic and reattached it to the earpiece. "Bobby? You copy?"

"I'm here."

"Good. See the target?"

"Yes, sir."

"Follow her."

CHAPTER TWO

Kenna surreptitiously pulled the top of the scarlet bustier higher. Why men went ape-shit seeing her boobs pressed beneath her chin was beyond her. Putting her private parts on display ranked right up there with a lap dance at a Chippendales show.

She stirred the glass of ginger ale, watching the fizz crawl up the red-and-white-striped straw. Bubble one burst before bubble two.

A sigh escaped. She didn't know if she had the guts to go through with this. Showing Jerry the sights had been one thing. Having Marissa set her up with a total stranger was something else entirely. It made her feel...well, cheap.

The backroom of Pedal to the Medal Saloon was filled to capacity. Most of the patrons were men—overweight, over the age of fifty. The young, good-looking, cocky ones preferred a more dangerous venue.

Immediately, Agent March popped into her head. He embodied danger. A sexy troublemaker that could short-circuit the logic center of her brain and rev her body into overdrive in six seconds or less.

The neon green Coors Light clock over the horseshoe-shaped bar read 9:15. She smirked and wondered if Mr. DEA was having fun at the fifth annual "Big Johnson" contest at the In-N-Out

Lizard Lounge. Kenna wasn't sorry she'd sent him on a wild dick chase, but she'd loved to have satisfied her curiosity whether his "Johnson" had a chance at the finals.

A fistfight broke out between two big-assed tattooed women while the sleazy object of their affections drunkenly cheered them on. The momentary distraction didn't alleviate the feeling she shouldn't be here for any reason. Especially not for money.

Marissa wandered by with a Hispanic guy, blindingly white teeth set against his pockmarked skin. In his mid-thirties, the man proudly wore the colors of a motorcycle gang—and about a million tattoos. Spooky, the way his flat brown eyes raked up and down Kenna's body like she was a particularly tasty burrito. She shook her head at Marissa, who detoured him toward the tequila bar.

Skynyrd blared. Pool balls clicked. Video lottery machines beeped. Conversations rose and fell. The masses of people were on vacation in world-famous Sturgis during Rally Week and were in the party mood.

Not her. She'd rather be flopped on her king-sized bed engrossed in the latest J.D. Robb novel.

Kenna propped her elbows on the sticky table behind her while she surveyed the room.

A gray-bearded ZZ Top look-alike swaggered by with a skinny dude sporting an orange bandana. She squinted at the table in the back where Marissa had returned and was holding court.

Whoo-yeah. Check out the guy with the killer ass.

A mountainous woman vigorously chalked her pool cue and blocked her view.

Come on baby, Kenna silently chanted to the man, *let me see if the front matches the back.*

As if feeling her intense gaze, the man turned.

Kenna nearly toppled off the barstool. Mr. Killer Ass was none other than Agent Drake March.

Shit.

His midnight hair fell in a sexy tangle around his angular face. He'd streaked the hair by his temples gray, making him appear older and sexier, if possible. A too-small black T-shirt clung to his defined chest and abs. Tight, tight jeans hugged his muscular thighs and yep…if the bulge beneath his button fly was real, then he definitely was a candidate for the "Big Johnson" award.

Grand prize division.

Irritating that he'd pulled off the biker garb. But he'd never be able to hide the cop attitude. Could he? When his gaze swept the crowded room she resisted the urge to duck.

Chances were slim he'd recognize her in a short black wig and brown contacts. She'd better not risk it.

She twisted her creaky stool around, feigning interest in the maraschino cherry sinking to the bottom of her ginger ale.

Less than thirty seconds later, hot breath seared the back of her neck. A sexual shudder ran the length of her body.

"I liked you better as a redhead, Kenna," he drawled.

Damn if her nipples didn't tighten. She pasted on a smile and faced him. "Well, if it isn't A—"

He covered her mouth with his. His big palm cupped her jaw, his thumb pulled her chin down, forcing her mouth open wider to meet his delicious onslaught. Sucking, stroking, licking, the kiss grew wetter, hotter and deeper with every arc of his talented tongue. Insistent kisses continually brushed seductively over her tingling lips and she couldn't break free.

After several dizzying seconds of destroying her composure, he drew back a little and murmured, "I'm not 'Agent' anything right now, so watch your smart mouth or you'll blow my cover. Call me Drake."

"Mmm," she purred, darting the tip of her tongue out for a quick taste of his full bottom lip. "How did you know I wasn't gonna say *asshole?*"

"Damn, you are a pain." He dropped his lips over hers hard, and the punishing follow-up kiss damn near scorched her tongue.

With her body a quivering mass, nothing mattered but the way this man made her feel: like an obsession.

Minutes, hours, days later, out of breath and out of her mind from such unrestrained passion, Kenna retreated. She pressed her forehead to his. "Stop kissing me."

"Stop letting me."

Drake's hands slid up the sides of her head, tipping her face back to meet his. "Jesus. One taste of you and I forgot how fucking mad you made me today."

"How did you find me? Maybe the question should be *why* did you find me?"

Those mesmerizing eyes changed from indigo to steel. "You know why."

"Uh-huh. You said I was free to leave after I answered all your questions."

His grip dropped to her shoulders. "I lied. And don't think I'm letting you out of my sight again. I'm still pissed off at you."

"Strange. Didn't seem like you were so mad a minute ago. I certainly wouldn't have pegged you for the kiss-and-make-up type, March."

She twisted away from him and saw Marissa headed straight toward them wearing a sour look.

Crap. Had she seen Agent March kissing her? She was supposed to be here checking out potential clients, not sucking face with a cop who wanted to ruin her life.

She was so screwed.

"Let. Me. Go."

"No. And not a word about who I am. I mean it, Kenna. You've pushed me far enough today. My cover name is Drake Mayhaven." He sidled in behind her, keeping his hands nearly around her neck, hard, hot and possessive.

Kenna gritted her teeth. Marissa had an uncanny ability to read situations and people. She wouldn't fall for his handsome face and lame attempts at charm.

Or would she?

Marissa, a striking brunette, turned heads as she crossed the room. She and Kenna lived in the same apartment complex. They'd been friendly, but not friends until last summer when Kenna's loose tongue had spilled the details of her financial woes over a six-pack of Corona at the community swimming pool. Off the cuff, Marissa had suggested Kenna tour her old friend Jerry Travis around Sturgis. Marissa claimed she knew women who made a killing acting as sort of an escort during the Rally.

Kenna had assumed Marissa had been joking.

She hadn't been.

In a moment of drunken logic, Kenna decided she had nothing to lose. Marissa worked in real estate and had convinced Kenna there wasn't any difference in renting rooms or renting people. Once Kenna sobered up, she'd tried to back out. But after she'd actually met shy Jerry Travis she'd almost felt sorry for him. Which is probably why she'd agreed to the bizarre situation and the chance to stay in school.

"Kenna. You going to introduce me to your friend?" Marissa asked sweetly.

Drake's left hand slipped down Kenna's bare arm. He threaded their fingers together while he reached his right hand toward Marissa. "I'm Drake Mayhaven."

"Marissa Cruz. See what happens when I'm late? Kenna makes all sorts of new buddies. So how did you two hook up?"

Kenna winced at Marissa's sly reminder that she was supposed to be hooking up with Marissa's friends, not making new ones on her own.

"Jerry Travis was a mutual acquaintance."

"Really? Seems he neglected to mention your name to me," Marissa half-chided.

"Must've slipped his mind. You know Jerry."

An unreadable emotion flickered in Marissa's dark brown eyes. "Pity about him. Were you two close?"

He shrugged. "We hung out. Did some business together."

"Yeah? Where?"

"Miami."

"Don't like Miami much myself." She frowned. "Wait a minute. Did we meet at Daytona? Perhaps at the Tiki—"

"Possibly. It's gotten to be nuts during Bike Week. Way too many people for my taste. That's why I decided to come to Sturgis this year. Jerry had planned on showing me the sights but Kenna's graciously agreed to do the honors. In Jerry's memory." His hand squeezed hers hard in warning.

"Of course. How thoughtful."

Kenna's teeth nearly bloodied her tongue when Marissa's eyes kept purposely cutting to the women's bathroom.

"Where you staying?"

bodies, beer bellies, flabby, wrinkled bare breasts, she saw the
glorious and grotesque firsthand.

A break in the crowd revealed her escape hatch.

She made a beeline for the back door. Sheer luck it stood wide open to clear out the gray clouds of cigarette smoke and body odors.

Once Kenna hit the cool night air she took a deep breath and ran like hell.

CHAPTER THREE

The dark area behind the bar resembled a modern day version of an Old West shantytown, with broken-down bikes, musty tents, overflowing garbage cans, blackened firepits. She dodged potholes and empty liquor bottles. Cursing the high heels, she darted between temporary storage units, a line of beat-up campers and rows upon rows of motorcycles.

After stumbling, she righted herself and zigzagged to the darkest, most deserted corner of the building. She'd hide until the coast was clear.

Nearly home free, Kenna thought right before a large hand clapped her on the shoulder.

Damn. Not enough air in her lungs to scream.

Double damn. Agent March was fast.

He yanked her arms behind her back and shoved her against a shed hard enough to get her attention. The metal—still warm from the heat of the day—bit into her cheek.

His labored breathing exploded across the back of her neck. "What the hell are you doing? You want to blow my cover?"

"I don't give a crap about your cover."

Agent March paused. Swore. Muttered something about his supervisor kicking his ass, then layered his hard body to hers, from hips to chest, settling his chin into the vulnerable bend of her neck. His warm breath seared her skin. A second later he tugged her earlobe between his sharp teeth.

Desire raced from that stinging spot straight to her core. Pathetic. How could she be turned on at a time like this?

"*Kenna Jones* might not care about my cover. But I'll bet you *Kaye Anne Ennis* does." He bit her earlobe again and laved the mark with a long, wet lick of his tongue.

She gasped. "How—"

"—did I found out who you really are?" His lips skimmed the fine hairs standing at attention on her nape. "I know all about you." He trailed his mouth along the slope of her shoulder. "Age: twenty-nine. Residence: apartment 17C at the Aspen Leaf Complex. Vehicle: a 1996 Ford Explorer, white. Occupation: doctoral candidate in geology. Want me to keep going?"

"You bastard."

"Yep. You shouldn't have lied to me, Kenna. But I tell you what. I'll let you make it up to me."

"This ought to be a stunning suggestion."

"Not what you think, cynical girl. Just act as my girlfriend for the next couple of days until I get the information I need on Diablo."

"Or what? You'll turn me in for solicitation?"

"No. I'll turn you in to the IRS for unreported income."

Tangling with the IRS was almost worse than the head of her department learning how she'd earned her tuition last year.

She was dead broke. Her grant application had disappeared again. Already up to her neck in student loans, she couldn't get another one at this late date. And to make matters worse, she'd been a victim of online identity theft. Until her financial mess was straightened out, no bank would even loan her a pen.

"No deal. If I'm helping you I lose my only chance to make some cash. Then I forfeit my place in the doctoral program."

He paused. "I can arrange to pay you."

Rage distorted her vision. She reared back until her head connected with his nose.

"Ouch! Goddammit! What the fuck is wrong with you?"

"I am not a whore."

"I know. I wouldn't be paying you for sex. You'd be paid as an informant."

"No difference."

Drake spun her around and loomed over her. Dangerous. Sexy. Ill-tempered. In short, an alpha male used to getting his way.

"Big difference. We will be working together."

"Not in this lifetime."

"Not negotiable, Kenna." His silky hair brushed her forehead when his soft lips grazed her ear. "But cheer up, there are other fringe benefits."

Her knees went weak, her fickle body softened. How was she supposed to resist him when he was so…overpoweringly male? "Like what?"

"Do I really have to spell it out for you?"

His eyes and his body silently spelled H-O-T S-E-X.

"I can't believe the federal government would condone this type of behavior."

"Not only does Uncle Sam condone it," he muttered thickly against her throat, "it is expected that we'll do whatever it takes to get the job done. Goddamn you smell good."

Kenna forced herself not to react to his bone-melting touches and shoved him away. "Including 'doing' me?"

"Yes. But don't play coy. You reluctantly agreeing to act like my girlfriend doesn't explain the chemistry that erupted between us from the moment I saw you."

She didn't deny it. There'd been an unusual, unexplainable magnetism drawing them together since the fateful moment they'd set eyes on each other at the Broken Arrow Campground.

His enticing lips moved closer. Hers parted in response.

To prove his point, he caught her face in his hands and leveled her with a brutal kiss. He explored every inch of her mouth. Slicking his tongue over her teeth, tickling the roof of her mouth, gently sucking her tongue. His lips were hard and then fleeting.

Kenna melted, losing herself in the way his long lean lines molded so perfectly to her lush form. The way his uncontrollable hunger made her feel wholly feminine and surprisingly secure.

Yet despite the soft tangle and retreat of his tongue, the strange rightness of his mouth controlling hers, she withdrew. Scared her to death, the sexual longings he brought to the surface.

Not to mention the power he had to screw up her life.

What the hell had she been thinking? She shoved him away. "Forget it. I-I have to go."

Drake asked mildly, "And where's the fire?"

"Besides in your pants?"

He smiled. "You put it there, hot stuff."

"You are a menace. I'm going back inside to tell Marissa this whole thing was a big joke."

His playfulness vanished. "I'm not laughing. You *will* be at that party with me even if I have to fasten one of those fancy rhinestone dog collars around your neck and muzzle you."

"You wouldn't dare!"

"Yes, I would. Be warned: if you try to run from me again, I'll break out the handcuffs."

"Forget it, perv." She threw her purse strap over her shoulder and spun on her heel.

Kenna didn't get far in those ridiculously sexy shoes. When she stumbled Drake caught her and whipped her back around.

His steel-toed boots bumped her sky-high red sandals and he completely invaded her personal space.

The little spitfire stood her ground. "Back off, March. I need time to think."

"No. You need to wrap your brain around the fact this is a goddamn federal case. You help me and I won't have you arrested. Simple. Doesn't take a doctorate to figure that one out."

"This sucks," she retorted.

"Yeah, so tough it up, doc. Enough stalling. Come on. We have things to do." He grabbed her hand and towed her behind him as he strode toward the parking lot.

She jerked him to a stop, digging into the hard clay despite the trash catching her high heels. "Where in the hell are you dragging me off to in such a rush?"

"My motel. I'll brief you and introduce you to my team."

"There's more of you?"

"How do you think we followed you today?"

"Damn devious government spies are everywhere," she muttered. "Hey, I thought you said you were staying at the Broken Arrow Campground?"

"We didn't know if we could get a room in Sturgis on such short notice. We kept the registration as a precaution in case anyone double-checks my cover."

"Are people chasing after you, Agent March?"

"Unlikely."

"But if they are—"

"For christsake, you think I haven't been doing this job long enough that I can't shake a tail?"

"Doesn't matter how good you are at chasing tail. I'm not staying in a sleazy motel room with you."

"Ha ha. You're fricking hilarious. You'd rather sleep in a tiny canvas tent with me and share a communal shower with a thousand other women?"

"What makes you think I'd want to stay with *you* anywhere?"

"Doesn't matter what you want. I'll be glued to your side 24/7. Get used to it. You're completely mine for the next few days."

"As your girlfriend? Great. I'm thrilled your partners will think I'm a pro."

"My partners know you're cooperating as an informant and are pretending to be my girlfriend."

Drake slowly traced a shadow from her defiant chin to the tops of her breasts. When she shivered, his smile evaporated. "No one has to know we're really lovers."

"You wish. Got all your bases covered, huh, slick?"

"I won't be covering bases, I'll be covering you. Don't tell me you haven't thought about our bodies slick with sweat, sliding, straining together in the dark. I can read the anticipation in your face right now." His thumb lightly brushed her full bottom lip. "We'll be lovers, Kenna. Soon. When it happens I won't be an agent and you won't be an informant. I'll just be a man and you'll just be the woman who's all mine."

Heat blazed in her eyes and she swallowed hard.

Not so confident now, Drake thought.

"This is crazy. I don't even know you."

"You will. You'll know me very, very well."

"You're pretty goddamn sure of yourself."

"About some things." He leaned closer. His smile grew bigger when her breath caught. "You react to the way I touch you. Even when you don't want to. Bugs the shit out of you, doesn't it?"

Kenna didn't answer. Her chin rose a notch. "Back to business, March. Which motel are you staying at? I'll meet you."

He laughed and shook his head. "Nice try, but no chance. I don't trust you."

"The feeling is mutual, pal."

Drake rocked back on his boot heels and waited, suspecting his silence would drive her crazy.

It did.

"God!" She gave him a frustrated look, growled and smacked him in the arm with her bulky purse. "You are such a control freak. Fine. We're going to my apartment first so I can get my stuff."

He smirked. "Good plan. I'll follow you."

"Don't think I'm leaving the door unlocked."

"I wouldn't dream of making such an assumption."

Her cat-like eyes gleamed. "Then is there a secret knock I'm supposed to know, Agent March?"

"No." Christ, she had a smart mouth. Maybe he was masochistic but it was turning him on beyond belief.

She granted him a cool once over, then rapped the rhythm "shave-and-a-haircut-pause-two-bits" on his chest. "Doesn't take a decoder ring to figure that one out, secret agent man."

Amazing that she didn't get whiplash from whirling away so quickly. He waited a beat, then caught her by her swishing hips, snaked his arms around her lithe body and clamped his lips to hers.

A token protest burst in his mouth before she kissed him back just as voraciously as he'd predicted.

This woman pushed his buttons. He pushed back. Oh yeah. They were so gonna set the sheets on fire.

Drake reluctantly released her ripe mouth an increment at a time. "Drive careful."

Kenna rolled her eyes and straightened her clothes. "Why? You gonna sic the highway patrol on me?"

"Smartass."

As she sauntered into the orange glow of the sodium lights, Drake suspected it might be easier to figure out who was behind Diablo than figuring out who was the real woman behind the different faces of Kenna Jones.

CHAPTER FOUR

Kenna watched foamy shower gel sluice down her body and swirl between her coral-tipped toes. Hot water relieved the aches in her muscles and the steam cleared her thoughts. Except for the dirty ones revolving around the hunky Agent Drake March, naked except for a wicked smile.

She'd escaped to the bathroom alone after letting him in her apartment. Even when his interest about conserving water had been apparent. Mostly in his jeans.

She'd packed hurriedly, locked the door, needing time to shed the trappings of Kenna—physically and mentally.

The man had knocked her for such a loop from his first touch she feared she'd never recover. The kisses in the shadows of the bar? Nothing short of phenomenal. Spontaneous. Passionate. Everything she'd heard a kiss could be but hadn't e xperienced firsthand.

His clever mouth, his naughty tongue, his demanding hands… Oh mama, what those hands could do.

In a hazy, dreamlike state, she imagined the rivulets of water racing down her body *were* his hard-skinned palms. Teasing her. Touching her lightly, but with intent. Liquid heat shot between her legs. Her breasts grew heavy. Nipples tight. Throwing her head back into the fine spray, she gave in to the uncontrollable driving need for release.

Kenna parted her lips and let droplets of water trickle inside as she remembered his dark masculine taste. The sensation of his velvety tongue sliding against hers. She imagined the heat from his muscular body would warm her bare skin as his large hands cupped and squeezed her breasts. He'd twirl her nipples, searching for that spark of pleasure that bordered on pain. She arched her back, pressing closer into the steamy water. Wanting more, wanting everything from this phantom lover.

His hungry lips would trail from her mouth to her ear. The soft, unintelligible words he'd whisper would send chills racing through her. He'd stoke her tremors of desire with each fiery touch from his hot hands.

He'd lick away the water flowing over her skin. His sharp teeth would score the column of her throat as he inched his way down her body. Nipping. Marking her flesh with tiny love bites. Then again his deft fingers would pinch and roll and tug her nipples until she cried out.

He'd laugh. Not cruelly, but with confidence.

She widened her stance and her hand slowly slipped across the wetness of her flat belly until it reached the moist thatch of curls.

Touch yourself for me, he'd urge.

No. I want you to touch me.

And in her fantasy, he'd obey.

Her ragged breath echoed in the tiny stall space. Cool water flowed over the smooth skin of her shoulders as her questing fingers parted the moist folds of her pussy.

Between the water and her juices, she was already slick. He'd murmur how hot it was that she'd gone wet and soft for him. Then he'd slide his middle finger up and down her slit.

Teasing her. Tormenting her clit until it peeked out from its hiding place.

She'd gasp as his rough thumb began to stroke little circles around that swollen nub. Back and forth. But it wouldn't be enough. Crazed with need, she'd bump her hips at him, an invitation for him to push a finger inside her.

He'd comply. One finger in. And out. Coated with her wetness he'd push even deeper on the second stroke.

Like that? he'd ask.

More, she'd demand.

He'd breathe heavily in her ear as he jammed another long, callused finger up inside her warm channel.

Yes. Don't stop.

He'd pump in and out in a primal rhythm that matched the thick throbbing of her blood. Lapping the sweat and water from her skin like it was liquid candy. Whispering how he'd taste the cream between her thighs and make her scream his name.

Kenna moaned, rubbing the plumped bud harder and aching to feel his thick fingers inside her, not her own.

She'd fill her lungs with his seductive manly scent as his soft hair tickled the sensitive curve of her neck. The rasp of his stubble would scrape her breast as he strongly suckled her nipple into his hot mouth. Deep enough the tip would hit the back of his throat.

The exquisite pressure of her own fingers thrusting inside her and the continual stroking of her clit pulled every internal muscle taut in anticipation. Her belly swooped and the spasms began. Water streamed down her face and into her open mouth as the detonation inside her body sent her freefalling.

Lights burst behind her lids. Blood pounded in her ears.

After the throbbing slowed, Kenna blinked the mist from her lashes. Whoa. She reluctantly removed her hand from her swollen sex, still feeling delicious little pulsing aftershocks. She squeezed her thighs together.

Stunned by the intensity of her orgasm, she fell back against the tile shower wall. Her shaking knees knocked over the shower gel, releasing the heavy aroma of gardenias.

If the real thing with Agent March was anything like her fantasies…

Geez. Talk about quick on the trigger. Hadn't taken her very long to get off. She snorted. When did it ever?

But what if he'd walked in on her?

So? the bad girl inside her countered. Would he have just watched her pleasuring herself with those steely blue eyes? Or would he have joined in?

Not only would he have joined in, he'd have taken over.

And would she have let him?

Well duh.

Kenna shook her head to banish the erotic thoughts. Water droplets splattered against the plastic shower curtain covered in daisies.

It'd be interesting to explore this potent attraction, which seemed equally baffling to him. Was it inevitable they'd do a little mattress dancing? Probably. Still, she had no intention of spending the entire week with him. She'd do her civic duty and get him into the private party, score a couple of primo orgasms. After that, he was on his own.

Would he really toss her in jail? Or call the IRS?

Most likely.

She shouldn't chance it. But she needed the money and would do anything to stay in school.

The water ran cold but she was slow to move, knowing he prowled in her apartment, waiting for her to emerge. The real her. No wigs. No makeup. No revealing clothes.

Why was she stalling? Afraid he'd prefer the brash, take-no-shit Kenna—who could make herself come in two minutes—to the demure, sexually repressed Kaye Anne? She climbed out of the shower, toweled dry and wiped the steam from the mirror.

For several moments she stared at her reflection.

With shaking fingertips she fluffed up the funky layers of her chin-length hair. The bronze highlights gleamed beneath the incandescent lights. She smoothed moisturizer over her face and squinted at the dark circles beneath her eyes. Definitely needed concealer. She slicked a coat of black mascara on her lashes. Better. But still nowhere near the glammed-up version Agent March had seen.

Kenna slapped on some gardenia lotion, slipped into her clothes and shoved her toiletries into her travel bag.

Taking a deep breath, she opened the door.

Drake stopped pacing around the miniscule antique dinette set the second the lock on the bathroom door clicked. He had to force himself not to run.

His size twelve feet moved pretty fast anyway. When he caught his first real glimpse of her, he skidded to a stop on the Berber carpet.

For christsake. She had freckles. Freckles!

Man. He was in so much trouble.

Kenna had propped her slim shoulder against the door jam and crossed her bare ankle in front of her other shin. Her elfin chin came up. Her eyes snapped defiance. "Well? You disappointed?"

Drake's mouth dropped open. "Jesus. Are you kidding me?"

Her hair was about a million different shades of blonde, brown, gold and red. Sassy, just like her. As he stalked closer he noticed that without all the face paint caked on, her skin practically glowed. Her smart mouth was the color of pink roses swirled in cream.

His groin tightened when he imagined sliding his cock in and out of that mouth. Finally he focused on her eyes.

That incredible lavender gaze stared back at him. Somehow he'd known those beautiful eyes were one hundred percent hers.

His hand cupped her neck. He brought her mouth to his. He kept the kiss easy even when his every instinct screamed to show her how frantic was his need to possess her.

"You're kissing me again," she said breathlessly.

"I know." A heady scent of sweet soap and warm woman lodged in his nostrils. Burned into his brain. "You smell like an exotic flower." Between flirty kisses he herded her toward the living area. "I'll bet you taste even better."

"Give me a break. I thought you were here to fill me in on the details of the case before we meet up with your partners."

Drake took a mental and a physical step back. Exhaled. "Fine. Sit down and we'll talk."

"You want something to drink?"

"No. Let's get this over with."

Kenna decided Agent March's rapid transformation from playful to persistent was nerve wracking. "Well, I'm thirsty. Be right back."

She snagged a bottle of lemon-flavored seltzer water and leaned against the kitchen counter to gather her thoughts.

Tick tick. Hum. The fridge kicked on. Green light glowed from the digital microwave clock.

The galley-style kitchen sparkled. She'd scrubbed black crud from the stove burner rings. The steel sink shone. The butcher-block countertop wasn't piled with junk mail and weeks-old newspapers. She'd even tossed the rotten carrots and mystery fruit from the veggie crisper. Good thing since she wouldn't be around for a few days.

Time to quit stalling. She pulled the garbage from underneath the sink and plopped it on the linoleum. Then she wandered back into the living room.

Drake had made himself comfortable on her chintz sofa.

She perched on the arm of the wing back chair. "So, what do you want to know?"

"The basics. Do you live alone?"

"No. I have a roommate."

"Who? Marissa?"

"No. Shawnee Good Shield."

He frowned. "Where is she?"

She squinted at the calendar. She had no idea when Shawnee would roll back into town. "On an archeological dig in Harding County. In the summertime she's only here a couple days out of the month."

"Does she know about Jerry Travis?"

"No." Shawnee would never have let Kenna go through with it last year. And if she'd found out Marissa was behind it… She shuddered to think how Shawnee would've reacted.

"Anyone besides Marissa know about your escort work?"

Her nose wrinkled. "It's not exactly escort work."

Pause. "Well, what is it?"

"Far out of the realm of my real life and personality."

He seemed to ponder her words as his gaze took in every nuance of her face. "What is your real life like, Kaye Anne?"

Acutely conscious of her damp hair and her face free of makeup, Kenna fought the urge to fidget. "First off. No one calls me Kaye Anne except my mother."

He grinned slow, easy, and oh-so-sexy. "She should've named you *Cayenne*. It suits you, hot stuff."

After the initial rush of pleasure from his flattery, she shook her head. "Wrong. Kaye is introverted and horribly bookish. Out of touch with the latest styles."

"I don't buy it." His introspective gaze swept over her conservative clothes. "There's more Kenna in Kaye than you're ready to admit."

She glanced at the sky blue sweatpants and matching camisole, complete with tiny satin bows and lace. Boring. Her original clothing choice—a funky red and white polka-dot halter sundress complete with shiny black "fuck me" pumps—hadn't looked boring. But she was afraid if she would've worn it Agent March might've believed she'd been dressing for him.

"I doubt the sexy number you wore earlier tonight fell from the sky."

"It fell on the floor actually." She smirked at his frown. "Online shopping at eBay is a godsend. Click. Five new mix and match outfits from the sexiest store around without having to stand in the glare of fluorescent lights and suffer through the attitudes of seventeen-year-old anorexic salesgirls. Plus it's cheap."

"So none of the leather, spike heels, low cut shirts and miniskirts are your clothing?" he asked skeptically.

Kenna smoothed a nonexistent wrinkle from the velour. "Kaye bought the stuff but Kenna wears it." Would he understand the difference between Kenna and Kaye? She enjoyed playing Kenna, even when that wasn't who she really was.

Or was Agent March right? Was she only fooling herself?

Her gaze drifted to the row of Snow Babies figurines symmetrically lined on the top of the entertainment center. For the first time in her adult life her choice of décor embarrassed her.

The urge arose to smash those sappy, happy pieces into shattered chunks of ceramic. Replace them with some risqué sculpture of engorged bronzed man parts or naked lovers entwined in a passionate embrace.

His sexy voice broke into her violent redecorating fantasy.

"It'll be easier if I keep calling you Kenna. No chance of mistakes that way."

"That's fine." She'd been thinking of herself as Kenna for days, anyway, in order to prepare herself. She blew out an aggravated breath. "I suppose you're ready to go."

Drake settled his muscular arm across the back of the mauve and crème floral couch. "In a minute."

She uncapped the bottle and drank deeply. Concentrated on the cool water rushing down her throat. When he continued staring intently, she snapped, "What?"

"You seem to know an awful lot about wigs, makeup and changing your appearance."

Agent March remained suspicious. Big surprise. "Didn't I tell you? I graduated from spy school. Same class as Sidney Bristow. Except she always got the hottest clothes."

He didn't crack a smile.

"Geez. Lighten up. I was kidding. My first foray into higher education was beauty school. At the Mystique Edge I learned the tricks of the trade."

"You still cutting hair?"

"Sometimes. Mostly for friends. On weekends I work at a couple of retirement homes, styling hair for little blue-haired ladies. Pays for my groceries."

His eyes moved over her, lingered on her unstyled hair and bare face. "Although you're hot as hell as a brunette and a redhead, I have to admit I like the way you look now the best."

She couldn't help it; she blushed. She didn't believe him for a second, though. "Yeah?"

"Yeah." Drake's nostrils flared, and he leaned forward, as if hoping to catch a whiff of her scent. "Damn if you don't smell sweet."

"I'm not very sweet-smelling when I'm out in the field. Not many showers at the sites."

His lips twitched. "Geology seems an odd choice."

"Not when you consider I'd gotten sick of being on my feet all day. Sick of the stink of permanent solution. Sick of the never-satisfied customers and the itty bitty paycheck."

"But why geology?"

"I dated a geological engineer for a while. Found out I had rocks in my head where he was concerned."

He laughed.

"Fell in love with geology instead of him. I still won't get rich, but my employment prospects are better." She scowled at the water bottle she'd inadvertently crushed in her hands. "Provided I actually come up with the tuition to finish my degree."

Drake shifted. He settled his strong forearms on his knees. "I told you I'd pay you."

"I know." Her gaze strayed to the quartz clock nestled between a set of blue geode bookends. "But that doesn't mean I believe you."

"Me specifically?"

The second hand on the clock counted off the time she was wasting. "No. It's just…I've waited for grants. Personally, and for the geology department. Requisitions don't mean squat to the government. Even if the appropriate agency does miraculously approve your request and decide to pay me, it may be months before I see a check. I need the money in my account now." As the words spilled out she knew she sounded incredibly callous.

"Kenna—"

Her gaze whipped back to his. "Don't try to placate me, March."

"I'm not."

"Good. Then if you've got enough dirt on me let's go."

Drake stood and bent to pick up her duffel bag, but she beat him to it.

"Hand it over," he said.

"Nope. You really want to help out, grab the garbage in the kitchen."

Grumbling, he slipped past her, returning with the tied white bag. "Anything else?"

"I've got everything I need."

She locked the door. They moved out the front entrance and down the stairs leading to the Dumpster.

Kenna shivered in her skimpy top. Drake trotted ahead, throwing back the plastic black cover and tossing the bag inside. The lid thumped. When she caught up to him something cracked beside her ankle.

Fearing a stray animal, she spun toward the sound. Looked down. Then another ping, closer, this time next to her hip. What the hell?

Confused, she looked at Drake.

He yelled, "Get down," and tried to shove her face into the concrete.

CHAPTER FIVE

"Goddammit, Kenna, get down!" Drake hissed, placing his palm on her head and pushing her to the asphalt.

She cursed, but stayed where he'd shoved her.

The stench of diapers, spoiled meat and rotten fruit registered before he automatically reached for the gun on his hip. Instead of the plastic grip of his Glock, his fingers connected with the smooth leather of his belt.

Fuck. Unarmed, zero back up and saddled with a civilian.

A fourth bullet pinged against the Dumpster. The fifth—a beat later—pounded into the container to their left. The sixth grazed the plastic lid on their right.

Nothing happened for several seconds…which crawled by interminably.

So they did have an advantage—the shooter couldn't pinpoint their exact location.

But for how long?

Drake couldn't outwait the bastard all night.

Sirens wailed in the distance. The utility light flickered, sending a strobe-like effect across the shadowed cement. A dog yipped and barked. The booming bass of a stereo reverberated from the parking lot before it was abruptly silenced.

He had no way of knowing whether the danger had passed and only one way to find out. Without moving his feet, he leaned over, placing his lips next to Kenna's ear. "You all right?"

Her chest rose and fell rapidly. She nodded.

"Stay put. I'll get my car. If I'm not back in ten minutes run to the manager's office and have him call the police, okay?"

"No. Don't go." Besides a quick shiver, Kenna remained motionless. One small hand clutched the duffel bag. Her violet eyes were big as saucers.

"I have to."

He studied the shadows, gauging which area would offer the most cover. A deep breath later he took off, aiming for a corner of the closest building. Sixteen steps and he flattened himself against the brick. Sweat flowed down his back in a river rivaling the Mississippi.

Silence. No shots rang out.

Adrenaline pumping, Drake crouched and ran the length of the complex, coming to an enclosed concrete courtyard where the sixteen units converged. Little cover there. The place was lit up like the Fourth of July. For security purposes it was great. For his intention to sneak around it pretty much sucked.

An eerie blue glow wavered from the community swimming pool. Three sides were enclosed by a redwood fence. He popped his head around the corner of one end, noticing the locked gate. Floral-printed chaise lounges stood empty. White resin lawn chairs were stacked. The striped umbrellas were tied shut.

The ceramic pots of petunias weren't large enough to conceal a poodle, so the shooter hadn't jumped the fence and hidden in there. Good. It'd be harder now for the son-of-a-bitch to get the drop on him from behind.

He listened to the sounds of the night. Traffic. The buzz of streetlights. Nothing out of the ordinary save the thumping of his heart. Ducking down, he scooted to the nearest edge of the parking lot, leaping from car shadow to car shadow on the balls of his feet.

While stopping to catch his breath, a car door slammed. He froze and hunkered against the rear wheel well of an oversized Dodge dually pickup.

Even though his pulse tripped, Drake forced himself to wait for the sweep of headlights. But the vehicle turned the opposite direction and didn't give away his position. His relief was short lived as two women approached and lingered by the rusted-out Honda next to him to chat.

If they saw him, they'd scream. If he showed himself as a precautionary measure, they'd scream. Either way he wished they'd stop dissecting some asshole's selfish attitude in the sack and get going or else *he'd* scream.

After they roared off, Drake stretched. His knees cracked like Rice Krispies.

He squinted. Across the back lot sat the black Jeep. The rental looked drivable. No slashed tires or broken windows. He frowned and dragged a shaking hand through his hair.

Why hadn't the shooter disabled his car? If they'd been following him, wouldn't they have tried to keep him from escaping?

Unless they'd showed up *after* he and Kenna had gotten here and had no clue what kind of car he'd driven.

Or…unless he wasn't the target.

Shit.

Drake moved quickly, not wanting to leave Kenna alone and unprotected another second. He slipped into the seat, shoved the key in the ignition, keeping himself from burning rubber to get to her.

He rolled up beside the Dumpster and reached back to open the door.

A wide-eyed Kenna launched herself into the rear passenger side. She held the camouflage duffel bag like body armor as she dove for the floorboards. Once she'd slammed the door, Drake sped out the back exit of the complex.

Conversation remained pointless as he drove in circles, keeping an eye on the rearview mirror. Soon as he was certain no one had followed them, he parked in the Save-Mart lot.

Curled up in the fetal position in the back seat, Kenna's body shook. Her pale eyes held the glassy sheen of shock.

"Hey," he said, stroking an unsteady hand down her arm. God. She was so cold. When he repeated the gentle caress, she recoiled. He managed not to flinch at her rejection. "You okay?"

Hysterical laughter bubbled out. "Okay? I'm f-f-ucking p-p-eachy. Th-thanks f-f-or asking."

He touched her again anyway. "Jesus. You're like a Popsicle." He twisted, intending to climb into the backseat with her. "Let me warm you up."

Kenna shrank further into the burgundy leather. "You just stay the hell up there and leave me the hell alone."

"Kenna—"

"Don't." Her mouth trembled but she firmed it. "I didn't ask for this. This is your fault. You dragged me into this."

Drake's gut clenched at her bitter tone. With more harshness than he'd intended, he said, "By involving yourself with Jerry Travis you got into this on your own."

"He's dead! I told you I don't know anything!"

In frustration, he threw up his hands and smacked the head-rest on the passenger's side. "Don't you understand? It's my job to investigate every avenue, even if it appears to be a dead end."

"Then am I a dead end?"

"Not any more."

Minutes ticked by. She measured him in silence and he was relieved to see she'd stopped shaking.

With a sigh, Kenna swung her sandals to the floor mat. She sat up and pressed her back against the door. "What aren't you telling me, Agent March?"

"What do you mean?"

"Why was someone shooting at you?"

Drake could act the big, macho man and spout something lame like this was all part of his job; it wouldn't be a lie. He decided to tell the truth for two reasons. First, Kenna needed to realize the severity of the situation. Second, if he pissed her off, maybe that anger would erase the dejection from her sweet face.

"What makes you think they were shooting at me?"

Everything inside Kenna shriveled in horror. "You think *I* was the target?"

"Yes."

"Why?"

"That's what I'm trying to figure out."

Her stomach roiled, snapping her fragile control. "For gods-sake, how can you even think they might've been shooting at me? You're a goddamned DEA agent. I'm a doctoral candidate. No one is trying to kill me for my thesis."

As soon as the words left her mouth, she froze. Had that jerk-off Trent somehow played a part in tonight's gunfire?

Kenna tried to blank the expression from her face, but Agent March caught it.

His shrewd gaze sliced into her like a laser. "Tell me who has a reason to want you dead."

"Not dead. Scared maybe." She nervously wound the purse straps through her fingers. "It's probably nothing."

"Let me make that determination."

"Last year my grant application never made it to the appropriate department. When I found out too late to apply for a student loan or an endowment, I thought I'd have to drop out of the program. And I panicked. During a moment of drunken stupidity I told Marissa. She offered to lend me the money, but I…I just couldn't *take* it, hence me earning it from Jerry Travis. Once I finally had the cash and paid the tuition—which was past due—I discovered this other guy in the program, Trent Eagle, had applied for and received the grant money. Instead of me."

Agent March stayed curiously silent. "How well do you know Trent?"

She squirmed. "He dated Shawnee for a couple months."

"He knew you were a grant recipient?"

Kenna nodded. "Our department is small. At first I didn't fault him for applying. I mean all's fair. But as the year wore on I suspected he'd done something to sabotage my application."

"Why?"

"Little comments he snapped off when he thought I couldn't hear him. Plus it made him psycho that my grades were better and the professors liked me because I'm not such a know-it-all asshole who plays the race card at every opportunity. Even with the financial help he nearly washed out and he's ineligible for the grant this year."

"So, realistically, he has a reason. He could've been the shooter."

"Unlikely. Trent's a wuss. He'd slash my tires or badmouth me, but he doesn't have the balls to do anything dangerous. Especially not to my face."

"You think he was responsible for your grant application getting messed up again this year?"

"Possibly. I told him if I found out he'd sabotaged my application I'd bring it up with the Dean of Students and the Financial Aid Office. Then he'd get kicked out for sure."

"Anyone else you pissed off lately? Another guy you 'toured' around the Rally?"

She bristled. *Tell him Jerry Travis was the only one,* but the truth stuck in her throat. "Me not riding around on the back of someone's Harley isn't a killing offense."

He'd focused his attention on a young couple quarreling over their screaming toddler as they unloaded diapers and beer into a beat-up beige minivan. "Who'd you meet tonight before I showed up?"

Kenna opened her mouth to tell him about the unsettling Mexican guy Marissa had almost brought over, yet something stopped her.

Drake turned, pinning her with a hard look. "Who?"

The coolness of his tone stung. "Some friend of Marissa's."

"Did you meet him?"

"Not personally."

"What'd he look like?"

Kenna described him the best she could remember. Her voice faltered as Drake's face remained blank as a statue.

"Did he have a spider tattoo on his left hand?"

The black and red image jumped into her mind's eye. "Yes, now that you mention it, he did."

He swore.

"What?"

"That was Tito Cortez. I'm assuming he's the guy who's having the party. His cousin Anson runs the Compadres. He's about third in line of the Compadres command structure. Jerry told me about him and Tito is loosely connected to some people I deal with in Florida."

She frowned. Where had Marissa dug Tito up? And why had her friend assumed she'd be willing to hang around with a thug?

"The Compadres have chapters across the country, including Florida, and are into everything from drugs to drag racing and strip malls to strippers," Drake added.

"Terrific."

He tilted his head from shoulder to shoulder. *Crack crack.* A grinding pop echoed and he groaned. "Move up front. Facing backward is giving me a serious pain in my neck."

"This whole thing is a serious pain in my butt," Kenna retorted.

"Too bad. Like it or not you're in this up to your ass. Since we don't know what's going on, at least if you're with me you'll be safe."

"Safe? Jesus! We just had people fricking shooting at us. How is that safe? Why am I even with you, March?" Dramatically, she smacked her forehead. "That's right. If I don't cooperate with you the IRS will come knocking. Or I'll end up in the Meade County jail for solicitation."

Drake brooded, forgoing his usual smart comment.

Her fingers clamped on the metal door handle, momentarily grounding her from this surreal scenario. She could leave if she really wanted to. Just jump out of the car and hide behind the potted palms in the Lawn and Garden Center until this all blew over.

Hah! And then what? If she'd didn't cough up the cash for tuition she'd probably end up wearing a blue smock and *working* at Save-Mart.

Wasn't like she could go home. Wasn't like she had anywhere else to go. Her parents had worked themselves to death on the ranch before the bank had foreclosed on it. Shawnee and Marissa were her closest friends. For now, she was stuck with Agent March. Not only was the situation alarming, her immediate primitive sexual reaction to everything about him scared the living hell out of her.

She sighed defeat. "Fine. I'll go with you. But after being shot at I'd almost rather take my chances with tax men than hit men."

He grinned. A full out you-rock-my-world kind of grin.

Kenna's heart did a slow somersault. God she was hopeless.

Dropping the duffel bag to the cargo area, she wormed her way up to the front seat and settled in.

Drake cupped her face in his hand. His thumb arced over her cheekbone in an effort to calm her. "We'll get to the bottom of this, Kenna. You'll be safe with me, I promise."

When the man wasn't annoying her he almost seemed like the type of guy she could count on.

She doubted it would last.

CHAPTER SIX

Drake found a spot in the jam-packed lot across from the old fashioned "motor" motel. Cheap, a little shady, perfect for blending in with the Sturgis Rally crowd. Since most places had been booked nearly a year in advance they were damn lucky they'd even gotten rooms.

Keeping Kenna shielded, he knocked on Geo and Bobby's room.

Through the chain, Bobby yawned, "Hey, boss, everything all right?"

"No."

Immediately the red door shut, the safety chains rattled and the door swung back open. Drake pushed Kenna inside first, followed and fastened the lock behind them.

Geo rubbed his eyes. "What time is it?"

"Midnight."

He groaned. "What's up?"

"Someone shot at us tonight."

Right away Geo snapped to attention and scrambled out of bed. "When? Where did this happen?"

"Outside Kenna's apartment complex about an hour ago."

Geo yanked a T-shirt over his bare chest. "Did you call the cops?"

"No." Drake placed his hands on Kenna's smooth shoulders. She immediately tensed.

"Bobby, Geo, this is Kenna. She's agreed to help us on this case."

She snorted. "Like I had a choice, Agent March." She shook hands with each man. "Do all you guys look like Cornhuskers linebackers?" Her gaze raked Geo and Bobby head to toe. "Bet you've got no problem going undercover as exotic dancers."

Geo grinned. Bobby's brawny chest puffed out beneath his flannel pajama top.

"Which one of you sneaky spy guys stalked me today?"

Bobby and Geo exchanged an amused look which for some reason set Drake's teeth on edge.

"Doesn't matter. Let's get everyone up to speed so we can all get some rest. Tomorrow is gonna be one long-ass day."

Kenna shuddered and wrapped her arms more securely around herself, seeming waiflike and lost.

Sensing her discomfort, Geo gallantly settled her in the only chair in the room. He tucked the gaudy flowered bedspread around her. Bobby asked if she needed a drink. When she declined, Geo asked if she was hungry.

Before either of them could offer her a massage, Drake snapped, "She's fine. Can we get to it?"

Kenna rolled her eyes. And if he wasn't mistaken, Bobby and Geo followed suit.

Drake launched into an explanation of the evening's events and a preliminary plan for the next day. Fifteen minutes later they were done.

"This is probably the only time you'll hear me say this, but go ahead and sleep in."

"Thanks for the consideration, boss," Geo said dryly.

Kenna's eyes had begun to droop.

"Come on. Let's get you to our room before you fall asleep."

Suddenly she was wide-awake. "Our room?" she repeated.

"Yeah, we're bunking together."

"I thought you were kidding!" She shot to her feet so fast she nearly fell flat on her face. With angry jerky movements she untangled the bedspread from her legs. "Get me my own room or I'm out of here."

"No. Deal with it."

"You deal with the fact I'd rather take my chances at *my* home in *my* bed with a sniper than have you breathing down my neck for the rest of the night."

"She can crash in here," Bobby offered quickly. "Geo won't mind switching."

"Shut up," Drake said. "You're not helping."

"I think we should consider Bobby's idea." Kenna sent him a shameless smile.

Big tough field agent Bobby blushed and stared at his size fifteen feet.

Jesus. She'd already wrapped him around her finger. If he left Kenna in Bobby's care he'd probably call her a taxi and lend her cab fare. Rookies.

"Don't you have any input in this, Geo?" she cooed.

Drake moved so fast she didn't have time to retreat. "Get one thing straight. This is my op. Until I say so, you're stuck with me. Everything changed when someone took shots at you, Kenna. It's my goddamn job to figure out who and why and what's at stake. That means you and I will be roomies for the next few days. Get used to it."

Kenna's chin came up. "Forgive me if I don't do the Snoopy dance."

Geo snickered until Drake glared at him.

"Come on." He reached for Kenna's bag, but once again, she slapped his hand away.

"Don't touch my stuff."

He went absolutely still. That was the second time she'd insisted on keeping him away from her bag. "Did you pack a gun in there?"

"Where's *your* gun?"

"In my room. I'm asking you again: Do you have a gun hidden in there?"

"No. But I'm perfectly capable of carrying my own suitcase, Agent March."

Inside, Drake exploded. Outwardly, he remained calm. God. He wanted to shake her. Grab onto those muscled arms and rock her back and forth until her luscious breasts spilled out of the flimsy camisole. Then he'd show her exactly what he was capable of.

"Well?" She hefted the bag and tapped her sandaled foot. "We going or what?"

Shit. He was acting like an idiot. An extremely horny idiot. "We're going."

His room was three doors down. Same setup as Bobby and Geo. Two double beds, a TV, a cheap-ass rickety table and one chair, also decorated in a blast of burnt orange and olive green.

Equipment covered the dresser. Clothes hung neatly in the closet. Luckily he hadn't left the stuff from his shaving bag scattered all over the tiny counter in front of the bathroom.

Drake braced himself against the wall while he toed off his boots. Wallet, leather pouch and keys landed on the bed.

Kenna dropped her duffel by the door and flopped on the bed closest to the window. She yawned and flipped back the covers. "I'm wiped."

"Aren't you changing into pajamas?" Visions of sexy night-gowns teased him; a frilly baby doll barely covering her gorgeous ass. A black silk nightie highlighting her dangerous curves. Or his personal favorite: nothing but fire flashing in her eyes and a "do-me-big-daddy" smile.

"No. I don't wear paj—"

"Even better. That way I know you won't be sneaking out."

She propped herself on her elbow and scowled at him. "Here's where you threaten to tie me to the bed."

Drake grinned. "Only if you ask me real nice." He yanked his T-shirt over his head and pitched it toward the chair.

"Don't hold your breath."

The barb didn't hold any sting when Drake noticed her eyes were glued to his chest. Hmm. No matter what her smart mouth said, her body didn't lie. Seemed she was the one having a hard time catching her breath.

He stretched, flexing the muscles in his biceps and contracting his abs. At the stunned, hungry look on her face he decided the hours spent in the gym were well worth it.

"What are you doing?" she croaked.

"Getting ready for bed."

Drake sighed, dropping his hands to his waistband. His fingers fiddled with the top button.

Then he unbuckled his belt.

Her gaze zoomed to his fly as he oh-so-slowly lowered the zipper. Damn if his cock didn't appreciate her rapt attention and offer an enthusiastic, hopeful salute.

She swallowed hard as he began to slide the jeans down his hips, inching them over his muscular thighs and past his knees.

"Enjoying the show?"

"God, yes," she responded eagerly before she caught herself. A faint blush stole across her cheeks, highlighting her freckles. She abruptly turned on her side.

Drake shucked his jeans completely off and stood there, feeling like an idiot with a hard-on pressing out of the top of his black boxers. "What? No goodnight kiss?"

"You can kiss my ass," she retorted.

"Careful, hot stuff. I might consider that an invitation."

"Go to sleep, perv. On your own side of the room in your own bed."

He laughed softly. "Goodnight, Kenna. Sweet dreams."

Kenna slowed her breathing, pretending to be asleep. Drake would probably start snoring any minute. Wouldn't that blow her fantasy of him straight to hell?

Oh yeah, he was man enough to fill a hundred fantasies.

She squeezed her eyes shut, but it was no use. Her brain insisted on reliving his sexy, impromptu strip tease. Over and over again until she'd memorized every damn detail.

His body boggled her mind. Long, lean and hard, muscled in all the right places—he definitely looked long and hard where it counted. Sweat beaded on her brow thinking about touching and tasting that tanned golden skin and corded muscles. Sifting her fingers through his unruly black hair. Taking his big cock in her hands. In her body. In her mouth. She suppressed a moan, but her body launched a rush of moisture south anyway.

Hell. She'd never get to sleep now.

A deep masculine grunt. Followed by a heavy sigh. The bed squeaked and the polyester covers rustled as he rolled over.

She stared at the warped pine paneling surrounding the window, then at the brownish water spots on the ceiling. Think of something not sexy.

Rocks. She smiled to herself and began to recite the geological periods. In order. By the time she reached the Paleolithic age, she'd relaxed enough to drift off.

Her sultry voice drifted to him in the dark.

"You asleep?"

Drake went absolutely still beneath the thin sheet.

She laughed softly. "I know you're awake, Agent March. I've heard you tossing and turning."

He sighed. No use pretending.

"Tell me something."

"What?"

"Is it hard to sleep with an erection?"

"What are you talking about?"

"Don't think I didn't notice you had a pretty impressive hard-on before you crawled in bed. I imagine you're still hard as a rock, aren't you?

"Kenna—"

"Can't be comfortable with that big thing poking you in the stomach. And I doubt you want to touch yourself with me in the room."

"Why—"

"Although you could sneak in the bathroom and jack off in the shower and I'd never know."

"What?"

"You heard me." The bedspread crinkled as she shifted on the mattress. "Every time you get in the shower, I'll think that's what you're really doing. Slicking your hands up with soap. Sliding up and down your shaft." She paused. "Who do you think about when you're stroking yourself?"

He didn't answer.

"An old girlfriend? A famous actress? Or a model? Think any of them know how to give a decent hand job?"

His heart started to pound. "Why are you doing this?"

"Because I want to know what you'd do if I wasn't here."

Jack off in the shower. Thinking of you the entire time.

"You really think I'll answer that?" She might talk tough but he doubted she could handle his answer.

"No. But since I am here I can give you the relief you're dying for."

He must have misunderstood her. He was so focused on how the fringed curtains stirred whenever the air conditioner kicked on that he didn't realize she'd moved until she'd slid beneath the sheets next to him.

"Kenna. I don't think—"

"Ssh. Don't think. Let me do this."

Her bare breasts were pressed on either side of his spine and her nipples were stiffened to hard points. When had she gotten naked? She plastered herself against him and he felt the curls covering her sex grinding into his ass. He groaned. His body was so hot it felt feverish. And the coolness of her silky skin against the heat of his nearly made him come right then.

She indulged in teasing nips along his shoulder until her naughty mouth connected with the curve of his neck. Her tongue flicked the fine hairs at the base of his skull. Sweet, warm breath drifted across his skin.

Drake shivered.

"Do you want me to stop?" Her delicate fingertips drew an idle path from his hip, up the ticklish bend in his waist to trace his pectoral. Circled his nipple. Trailed back down. While driving him insane with fleeting caresses on his overheated skin, she writhed against his back. Did the thought of him exploding in her hand make her hot?

"Drake? What's it gonna be?"

"Don't stop."

"Mmm," she hummed against his shoulder blade. "I like the way you smell." She walked her fingers over the edge of his hipbone to his groin. No tentative touches. Kenna wrapped her hand around his rigid cock and pumped from root to tip. "I like the way you feel."

He arched his hardness into her soft hand.

"Do you want me to tease you? Make it last longer?" Those wayward fingertips delved into the hair covering his sac. She rolled his balls between her fingers and used her thumb to stroke the pulsing vein running up the length. Then she circled the base of his cock with her forefinger and thumb and squeezed. "Well?"

"No. Don't tease."

Her breath cascaded over the sweat gathering on his spine. "I wouldn't dream of it." Kenna slid her hand back up, tightly curled her fingers around his thickness and began to work him.

Pure unadulterated pleasure flooded his brain. "Ah. Jesus that feels so fucking good."

She kissed the spot below his ear. "Imagine how good it'll feel when it's my wet mouth on you instead of my hand."

"You really want to make me come fast, don't you?"

A confident feminine laugh. Then she started a blissfully brisk rhythm that made him groan and thrust higher to meet her masterful strokes.

Twisting up to the tip. Down to the root. Over and over. No change in the pace. Her touches were oddly familiar.

Kenna seemed to know exactly what he liked. How hard she could pull on his dick without making it painful. How much he craved the pad of her thumb circling the plump head with each upstroke. Each tug brought him closer to the edge. He held his breath. Clenched his ass cheeks, bumping his hips and closed his eyes, readying himself to burst in her hand.

God. It was right there. That ultimate rush of relief…

Then she started snoring.

He froze. His cock twitched at the sudden loss of friction. What the hell? How could she fall asleep at a time like this? When he was so goddamned close?

He opened his eyes. Looked down.

And saw *his* thick fingers wrapped his stiff cock, not hers.

Fuck. His stomach muscles tightened. Had it all been a wet dream?

Dawn approached, chasing away the dark shadows of the room. Drake rolled slightly, cringing when the bed squeaked. He shot a nervous glance her direction, zooming in on her form on the other bed.

She had one pillow over her head. Her spine curved toward him and he saw the Victoria's Secret tag sticking out of her camisole. A slender, bare calf peeked out from beneath the white sheet. Good. She had her back to him. Her loud snort bounced off the cheap paneling and echoed in the small room.

He slumped with relief. She was still asleep. At least she hadn't realized he'd been whacking off in the bed right beside her.

Talk about pathetic.

Then he realized he hadn't moved his hand. He glanced down at his cock. The purple head was swollen and his shaft was an angry red. Unhappy with the interruption.

No shit. He sighed and yanked up his boxers. Pity to waste a good hard-on.

Looked like he really would be taking his relief in the shower by himself. Again.

But he knew exactly whose face he'd be picturing.

CHAPTER SEVEN

Drake was gone the next morning when she woke up. The shower walls were still beaded with moisture. The humid air in the bathroom carried his scent so Kenna knew he hadn't been gone long.

She cursed as she untangled the snarly red wig. After securing it on her head, she brushed the flyaway strands, scrutinizing her appearance in the bathroom mirror.

No contacts today, just heavy black eyeliner. Fake mole on her cheekbone. She'd made her nose appear thinner and longer with pencil shadowing. Red eyebrows. Bubble-gum pink lips. She removed fuzz from the sequined black Harley Davidson tank top with a lint brush. Peeled on a black spandex mini-skirt.

The door to the room slammed. Agent March had returned.

Her stomach jumped. She tossed out knee-high patent leather stiletto boots and her purse, lugging the packed bag behind her as she exited the small space ass first.

"Agent March, you think we can swing by—"

A sharp intake of breath froze the words in her throat.

She glanced over her shoulder.

Bobby stared, glassy-eyed, slack-jawed, his cheeks a charming shade of pink. He shuffled his feet with enough vigor the shoelaces came untied. "Umm…morning, Ms. Jones. Agent March had to double-check some equipment and he asked me to—"

"Stay here and baby-sit me?" She gave Bobby an apologetic smile. "Sorry. Get a bit edgy before my first cup of coffee."

Bobby brightened. "There's coffee in the lobby. I could get you a cup if you'd like."

"You are so sweet," she cooed. "Two creamers, no sugar."

"Be right back." He spun on his tennis shoe and darted from the room.

Kenna grinned. If it ever came down to it, getting around Bobby wouldn't be any problem. Agent March? Damn near impossible. The man's instincts were unparalleled.

After Bobby returned, she reclined on the bed, sipping the strong, bitter brew. She wiggled her bare toes thoughtfully. "Do you prefer red or pink polish on your girlfriend's toenails?"

"Umm…"

"Don't tell me you haven't noticed! Do you know how hard it is to keep feet and toes sexy? Especially in the summertime?" Not that she spent much time grooming her feet, but it suited her purposes to let Bobby think she was a girly girl.

Bobby blushed and stammered, "P-pink I guess."

"So do you think this color is hideous?" She pointed her toes ballerina style. "You can't see it from there. Come closer." Bobby's eyes went round with alarm, but he reluctantly sidled over. "Think I oughta paint them pink?" Kenna frowned. "Does it look like the polish on the big toenail is chipped?"

He peered down and squinted. "Which one? Left or right?"

"Either."

"I can't tell." Bobby dropped to his haunches for a better inspection and warily lifted her right foot.

Of course, Drake chose that moment to barrel into the room.

"What the hell are you doing, Bobby? Giving her a pedicure?"

Bobby jumped like a spooked cat. "I-I—"

Drake's gaze zoomed to the Styrofoam coffee cup clutched in Kenna's hand. "Where did you get that?"

Poor Bobby froze like a trapped animal.

Kenna answered breezily, "We walked to the lobby. Why? Am I a prisoner? Am I not allowed to leave the room, *boss?*"

A beat passed as Drake stared at her. "Out," he growled at Bobby.

After Bobby's hasty departure, she scooted to the edge of the mattress. "You are so rude."

"You are so testing my patience." He tossed her boots on the bed. "Put those on. I'm ready to go."

"Well, la-di-fucking-da. I'm *not* ready to go. If you haven't noticed, I'm enjoying my breakfast."

"I'll feed you, okay? After you finish getting dressed."

"I am dressed."

"Then put on your damn shoes so we can go."

Kenna sipped, studying him over the rim of the cup.

Fifteen seconds later, he exploded. "You purposely trying to mess up my schedule?"

Yes. "No." She drained the coffee and pitched the cup at the garbage can. Stretched. Checked her fingernails.

"Then put your boots on!"

"You want my boots on so badly, Agent March, why don't you put them on yourself?"

An unholy gleam lit his eyes. "Great idea." He dropped to his knees, circling her ankle with his big hand.

"I was kidding!"

"Never offer a dare if you're not prepared to follow through, Kenna."

Watching her expression, he sucked her pinky toe into his hot mouth.

Kenna gasped. Fire shot from that toe straight between her thighs.

Hello foot fetish.

Drake hungrily sucked each toe while lazily gliding his fingertips up and down her calf in a mesmerizing manner that made her very glad she was sitting down.

His eyes never left hers. Finally, he reached for the boot, unzipped it and eased her foot inside. Those tantalizing lips softly brushed the inside curve of her knee as he zipped it up. "Need help with the other one?"

"No!" How much torture could she stand? But when a very male, very satisfied chuckle rumbled against her thigh, she decided revenge would be sweeter than outrage.

Kenna shoved him. A surprised look crossed his face as he fell on his ass. As he clambered to his knees, she arched her back and spread her legs. Wide enough that nothing was left to the imagination.

His gaze zoomed to the gap in her skirt. Narrowed. His nostrils flared. "Jesus, Kenna. Are you even wearing underwear?"

"Why don't you take a closer look to satisfy your curiosity?" she purred.

Drake crawled across the shag carpet until his heavy breath tickled her legs. He inhaled deeply and shuddered. "Wouldn't take much for me to rip that thong aside and set my mouth on you."

"No, it wouldn't."

"Would you let me?"

"Let you what?"

"Bury my tongue inside you? Lick you until I've tasted every secret inch of that sweet smelling pussy?"

Kenna didn't answer.

Taking her silence as acquiescence, he palmed her knees, opening them wider yet.

Despite the need pulsing through her, she fisted his soft hair in her hands, forcing his gaze to hers and away from her crotch. "Since you were in such a hurry, Agent March, you'd better hand me my other boot. We wouldn't want to keep your partners waiting, or mess up your precious schedule."

Right. What a lie. To hell with Geo and Bobby. Every pulsing nerve in her core ached for the exquisite sensation of his tongue fulfilling the decadent promises his mouth had made.

She wasn't sure, but she thought he whimpered.

He stood, wiping the sweat from his brow. "You fight dirty."

Her triumphant smile stayed in place as she zipped up her boot. Guaranteed he'd think of a suitable payback.

Kenna stood on shaky legs and snagged her purse. "Let's ride, Agent March."

No mistake. Drake really did groan that time.

••

Even with the motel located a mere mile from downtown Sturgis it took damn near forty-five minutes to reach Main Street. Drake cut the engine on the Harley and parked, searching for a landmark to locate their bike among the thousands of others.

Motorcycles in every color of the rainbow lined the middle of Main Street as far as the eye could see. Chrome reflected in bright, shiny spots on the scorching pavement as the blistering August sun beat down.

He climbed off the bike and steadied it as Kenna gracefully swung her leg over the seat, giving him a brief glimpse of her black thong.

While she adjusted her clothing, he relived the agonizingly slow bike ride. Her bare legs sliding along his thighs. Her smooth arms locked tight around his torso. The soft swell of her breasts pressed into his spine.

God. At one point he smelled her arousal as her groin rubbed against his ass whenever they stopped. Every time he'd stepped on the gas and the Harley's seat vibrated, her breathy moans echoed in his ear.

His dick was so hard he could've used it as a kickstand.

She patted her head, making sure the wig had stayed in place and slid pink sunglasses higher on her nose.

"The Back Door Saloon is about two blocks down."

"Why are we going there anyway?"

Drake pocketed the keys. "I'm meeting someone."

Her sharp gaze pierced him even through her dark shades. "Was this a prearranged meeting?"

"Yes. I don't have time to explain." Nor could he tell her what was going down. He snagged her hand and pulled her along behind him.

They wended through the people clogging the sidewalk. Most everyone wore black and the crowd rippled with energy. Heat rose from the sidewalk, making it impossible to breathe. They bypassed the Hooters tent and a leather vendor specializing in bondage gear. When Kenna stopped to check out the wide selection of cock rings, Drake dragged her away.

A leggy brunette—her size 46DDs bursting from a microscopic snakeskin bikini top—had draped a ten-foot python across her tanned shoulders. She blew him a kiss and crooked her finger at him with a come-hither smile. He shook his head. So far Sturgis had lived up to its name.

Above the entrance to the Back Door Saloon hung a sign, "Ladies: A Free Beer for a Free Show."

Kenna's lips tickled his ear. "I am not showing my tits to every pervert in the bar just for a free Coors Light, Drake."

He turned so they were only a breath away. "I wouldn't dream of asking." He lightly brushed his mouth over hers. "And I don't share," he said, sinking his teeth into her fleshy bottom lip. He immediately licked away the pain of the sting, tasting the sweetness of her lipstick and the sharper taste of her desire.

They stared at one another. A smart retort was slow in coming.

Drake scanned the vicinity. No sign of Geo or Bobby. Trying to park a van near the main drag in Sturgis was worse than cruising in on a bike.

Much as he hated it, he'd have to leave Kenna alone. He couldn't risk blowing the cover of the local DEA agent waiting for him inside the bar.

"Look. You hang around out here for half an hour or so and get something to eat. Let me do my business inside and then we'll wander Main Street for awhile." He fished a crumpled fifty from his left pocket and pressed it in her palm.

Those pink lips flattened into a grim line. "Why did you drag me along if you planned on ditching me?"

"I'm not ditching you. Bobby and Geo are supposed to be here but they must've gotten stuck in traffic." When several beats passed and she didn't make a smart-ass remark, he said, "What?"

"You are an asshole. And I don't need your money." She let the bill flutter to the ground.

Talk about touchy. Drake bent to pick it up. When he straightened, Kenna had vanished into the sea of black.

"Fuck." Out of options and out of time, he headed inside the dark smoky bar. He'd deal with her later.

Kenna leaned against the side of the building, trying to control her temper. The man was infuriating. Not only didn't he need her there, he didn't want her there. Why the big hustle to get ready?

If she asked questions he'd evade. Made her want to scream. Did he just expect her to follow along with everything like an obedient little lapdog?

Yes. So far she had.

Scents of cigarette smoke, meat fried in onions and the sugary scents of mini-donuts wafted over her. Didn't make her hungry. The greasy blend of odors made her stomach roil.

Or was her naivety causing her to feel sick?

Doubts rushed in. How much did she know about Drake March? If he was DEA, why hadn't he shown her a badge? Wouldn't the real DEA knock down her apartment door with a battering ram instead of arranging a fake meeting via a decoy email account?

Even Geo and Bobby's presence could be easily explained. Hired men. Private security companies had access to the same gadgets as the government. Odd, that they called him "boss", not Agent March.

What if none of them were DEA? What if they were members of a Miami drug cartel trying to find out how much Jerry Travis had told her about Diablo?

God. What if they'd cut her off from everyone because they intended to kill her when she no longer proved useful? What if his deliberate attempts at seduction had been the easiest way to ensure her compliance?

Despite the midday heat rising from the asphalt, her blood ran cold.

Kenna inhaled a couple of calming breaths. Deep enough to dig her shoulder blades into the cement blocks of the building that held her up.

Okay. All she had to do was get to a pay phone and call Shawnee. Shit. Shawnee wasn't around.

She'd call Marissa. With her real estate contacts, she'd have access to a place to hide her until this blew over. Or she could help her contact the local authorities and see if Drake March or Drake Mayhaven, or whatever the hell he was calling himself, really worked for the DEA.

She cut through the mob, ignoring the vendors shouting enticements. Grilled rattlesnake? Eww. Twenty percent off "intimate" body part piercing? Double eww.

It was harder to ignore the stunning young women wearing flesh-colored pasties and thongs, posing with any man who'd pony up a cool ten bucks. How could they sell themselves…she skidded to a stop.

Omigod. She'd taken money from a strange man for the pleasure of her company. How was that different?

It wasn't.

Before Kenna submerged herself into more self-recrimination, she caught a glimpse of a curtain of long hair, thick and shiny as a slab of black onyx. Only one person in the world had hair like that.

Shawnee.

When the woman flipped her mane back and tossed a rainbow-beaded purse over her shoulder—a purse identical to the one Kenna carried—she knew it was her roommate hustling through the biker crowd. But why?

Kenna's pulse quickened. What the hell was Shawnee doing in Sturgis? Kenna knew she occasionally helped out a friend in one of the bars, but Shawnee was pretty mum on which one. Besides, Shawnee was supposed to be on a dig in Harding County.

It didn't matter. Kenna was relieved to see her. She yelled, "Hey, Shawnee! Wait up!"

Shawnee stopped and turned. She looked around frantically, her gaze zooming from one unfamiliar face to another. Suspicion had drawn her mouth tight. Not once did that skittish gaze land on Kenna. A look of absolute fear distorted Shawnee's beautiful features before she slipped on a pair of sunglasses, whirled back around and vanished into the swarm of people.

Kenna froze in the middle of the sidewalk.

Shawnee had blown her off. Some best friend.

Then it hit her. Shawnee wouldn't have recognized her, all dolled up as biker bitch Kenna. No wonder Shawnee had panicked. Shawnee purposely kept a low profile, given her checkered past—and she was justifiably paranoid around strangers, especially avoiding the types of people with sketchy pasts much like hers.

Shawnee was probably halfway to Whitewood by now, that girl could run like the wind. So…what did Kenna do now?

Plan B. Call Marissa.

A blue pay phone shone in the sun like a beacon. Kenna hustled toward it, digging in the bottom of her purse for change. Shaking fingers punched the number to Marissa's cell. *Please, please pick up.*

"Marissa Cruz," she said brusquely.

"Marissa! Thank God. I-I—"

"Kaye? I mean Kenna? What's going on? Where are you?"

Motorcycle engines revved and she raised her voice. "Downtown Sturgis, at a pay phone across from the Circle S. Please. I need to talk to you in person. Is there any way—"

"Hang on." Marissa's words were garbled as she spoke to her companions. "Okay. I'm back. I just finished showing a building at the end of Lazelle Street, about four blocks from you."

Relief made Kenna slump against the phone box. "Can you meet me here?"

"I'm on my way." She chuckled. "What color is your hair today, *chica?* So I know who to look for?"

"I'm wearing the red wig. Oh and I dressed in black."

"That ought to be easy to spot," she said dryly. "Hang tight." She broke the connection.

Distracted, Kenna paced. Wondering how the hell she'd ended up in this crazy situation. Stuff like this didn't happen to her. She'd nearly made the fourth pass past a garbage can crammed with beer bottles and crumpled up food wrappers, when a sharp jerk separated her purse from her shoulder.

For half a second she froze, watching the black knit cap and leather jacket bobbing and weaving through the crowds with her purse held high above like a trophy.

In the next instant, Kenna was running after him.

Anger, fear, adrenaline, whatever it was, she seemed to be gaining on the punk. Pounding the concrete in her stiletto boots sent shock waves up from her heels through her shins, but didn't slow her down. Keeping her gaze firmly fixed on his head, she bulled her way through the throngs of people.

Almost. Not quite. Finally close enough. Releasing a primal scream, she tackled him. An all out flying leap that knocked both of them to the hot, sticky pavement. They landed in a tangle of arms and legs.

Her knees hit first, then her forearms, then her elbows. Her face smacked into a hard thigh, but not before she saw her purse fly from the assailant's hands and skid a few feet to her left. Despite having the wind knocked out of her, she scrambled sideways and lunged for it.

Yes! When the straps were firmly in her grasp, she looked over her shoulder.

The dirty rotten thief had disappeared.

At least the bastard hadn't gotten away with her favorite purse. And her wallet. He'd put a serious dent in her dignity however. She slowly settled back on her knees, attempting to literally cover her ass.

"Ma'am? You okay?" A silver-haired man and his equally silver-haired female companion had hunkered down beside her, wrinkled faces heavy with concern.

Kenna managed a small, "Ooof."

They assisted her to her feet amidst the leering crowd, who'd given them a wide berth but no offers of help.

The sweet little old lady—who sported a baggy fuchsia leather halter and matching leather hotpants—gently tugged Kenna's Lycra skirt down from her hips. She readjusted her tank top and clucked over the scrapes just starting to bleed.

The man muttered, "Sad, when you aren't even safe in broad daylight in South Dakota."

"Thanks for helping me." Kenna's body began to pulsate with pain. Spots danced in front of her eyes, distorting her vision.

"Sweetie, you really should go to the first aid station."

"She really ought to go to the cops," the man grumbled.

"I'll be fine in a minute." She closed her eyes and staggered backwards. "I'm waiting for a friend."

"Kenna!" Marissa's panicked voice cut through the air. Strong hands steadied her. The familiar scent of patchouli soothed her. "Oh God! Honey, what happened?"

"Purse snatcher." She grimaced when shooting pain zapped her in the head. "Failed attempt, fortunately."

"Where are the police?" Marissa demanded.

"That's what we wondered."

Marissa took charge and reassured the worried older couple. "It's okay. I'll make sure she's taken care of. Thank you."

Kenna peeled her eyes open, one lid at a time. "I just need to sit down." She stumbled toward the wooden bench facing the street.

Marissa muttered and plopped next to her, handing over a bottle of water. "Drink this. You look like you're gonna pass out, *chica.*"

"Feel like it too." She drank, careful not to guzzle it all at once, lest she add throwing up to her public humiliation. "I can't believe this happened to me on top of what happened last night."

"What happened last night?"

She took another sip. "After we left the bar, someone shot at us at the apartment complex."

Marissa gasped. "*Shot* at you? Are you sure?"

"Yep."

"Why?" A total expression of bafflement deepened the frown lines between Marissa's eyes.

"I don't know."

"Where did you go after someone shot at you? To the police station?"

"No. I went with Drake."

"To the campground? Dammit, you could have stayed with me. Why didn't you call me last night?"

Kenna hedged. "Because I was really freaked out. I'm still freaked out. That's why I called you today. This whole thing with Drake…I don't know if I trust him, even if he supposedly was a friend of Jerry's."

A soft hand stopped her from taking another drink. "I'm glad you called me. I've been worried sick about you and this Drake person."

When Marissa didn't elaborate, Kenna said, "Why?"

"Don't get mad, but I don't trust him either." Marissa expelled a heavy sigh. "I learned some pretty disturbing things about my so-called friend Jerry when I went to Daytona this spring. So disturbing, in fact, I told him there was no way I'd let you hang out with him during Sturgis this year. No matter how much money he offered. I cut all ties with him shortly afterward."

Kenna's stomach rolled over. But she'd kept in touch with Jerry via email without Marissa knowing. Crap.

"Then he wound up murdered." Marissa shivered. "I wish I'd known what kind of person he'd become. He was always so sweet and harmless when we were younger." Marissa's enormous brown eyes shimmered with tears. "I'm so sorry. I've been such a lousy friend. And when this guy showed up out of the blue, claiming to be a buddy of Jerry's…I didn't want to tip him off that I knew what kind of guy Jerry really was. He was so determined that you show him the sights…and I couldn't get him to leave so I could talk to you alone." She sniffed and reached in her purse for a Kleenex. "This is so unbelievably screwed up."

"It's not your fault."

"Yes it is! Don't you think it's suspicious that all this bad stuff has happened since he showed up?"

Maybe Marissa was on to something. Kenna felt those niggling doubts come back full force.

Her gaze sharpened. "And where is this Drake guy now after some thug tried to steal your purse?"

Kenna pointed to the seedy bar kiddy-corner from where they sat. "He had a meeting at the Back Door Saloon."

Marissa slumped back into the bench and wouldn't meet Kenna's quizzical gaze.

"What?"

"Nothing."

"Come on, tell me, Marissa."

"Fine." Folding her arms over her chest, her tone was cool. "The Back Door Saloon is rumored to be the place to make deals without the cops' interference."

"As in drug deals?"

She shrugged. "That among other things."

"How do you know all this?"

"My friend Angela used to work there as a bartender. She's told me some things about that place that'd set your hair on end. Stay out of there and stay away from anyone who admits to doing business there."

While Kenna digested the information, she watched the gleaming motorcycles parading up and down Main Street. The rumble of engines, the smell of exhaust, the dry heat. Gave her a headache. Every muscle in her body throbbed. She glanced down; her knees were bleeding. She wanted to crawl in bed—her own bed—and sleep until the pain went away. She thought about the Excedrin and everything else in her duffel bag back at the motel. "I don't suppose you've got any aspirin?"

"Yep. In my line of work I need it every day." Marissa rummaged in her Coach purse, coming up with two white pills.

Kenna popped them in her mouth and gulped the last of the water. "Since someone shot at me I can't go home. Got any suggestions on what I should do now?"

Before Marissa answered, a shadow fell across the bench.

Kenna didn't have to look up to know Drake had found her.

Chapter Eight

"What is going on? For christsake, Kenna, you're bleeding!"

Drake bent down, gingerly tracing the soft flesh beside the gash on her knee. He examined the matching cut on the other knee and the rivulet of blood running down inside the leather boot. Hell. He'd left her alone for thirty minutes, max.

He glared at Marissa. "What are you doing here?"

"Maybe the question should be where were *you* when some asshole tried to snatch her purse?" Marissa retorted.

Jaw tight, his gaze flickered to the rainbow-beaded bag nestled in Kenna's lap before he focused on her pale face. "Tell me what happened."

"I was standing here, minding my own business when some jerk-off grabbed my purse and ran. I tackled him. He didn't get my bag, but when I turned around the slimy fucker had vanished." She frowned and twisted her arm, checking the damage on her elbow. "Bastard. I hope he's bleeding."

Drake gaped at her. What had possessed her to tackle someone? Especially a guy? No wonder she'd been beat to shit.

Marissa murmured in Kenna's ear.

Kenna shook her head vigorously and groaned in pain.

Marissa straightened up and faced Drake. "Kenna will make lousy company today. I'm taking her home. I'll bandage her up and make sure she gets some rest."

"The hell you are."

Kenna's eyes widened.

Was it an illusion, or did his informant suddenly seem afraid of him? Great. Just fucking great.

"Watch it, Mr. Mayhaven," Marissa said crossly. "I don't know what your game is. Frankly, I don't care. However I do care about Kenna and since she's met you she's had nothing but problems."

"Let me tell you something, Ms. Cruz—"

"Enough." Kenna made a time out sign. Her hand covered Marissa's and she squeezed. "Thank you. But I've got to go with him to pick up my duffel bag. All my stuff is there."

"And then what? You're not staying with him at the campground?"

Kenna didn't answer.

Drake watched some mental communication pass between them. Gave him a weird vibe he didn't like one bit.

Marissa hugged Kenna and said, "Promise you'll call and let me know how you're doing. Promise me. I mean it. No matter what, you have to call me."

"I promise."

She stood. Flicked her long brown hair over her shoulder as she spun on her navy pump and melted into the crowd.

Kenna slowly rose to her feet. "I need to get this blood cleaned up. There's a first aid station on the next block."

When she wobbled, he caught her. "Want me to carry you?"

"And make a bigger spectacle of myself than I already have? No thank you." She shrugged off his assistance and tottered down the block in her sexy boots.

Damn stubborn woman. She wouldn't even let him inside while an EMT tended to her.

Racked with guilt, he paced outside the medical tent.

A stick-thin teenage boy sat on the folding chair. An angry red road rash stretched from his elbow to his shoulder. Next to him, a shirtless, bloated Jerry Garcia clone held a bloody towel to his recently broken nose. His old lady chewed his ass for fighting again.

Where the hell had Bobby and Geo been? They were supposed to keep an eye on Kenna. Coupled with the gunshots last night, he had a hard time believing she'd been a random mugging victim today.

But who could possibly want to hurt her? And why? What wasn't she telling him?

An EMT led Kenna through the tent flap. Drake rushed to meet her, forgoing the urge to fold her frail body in his arms. "Is she okay?"

"Not the worst I've seen this week." The stout African-American woman wagged her finger in his face. "There a reason she hasn't had anything to eat today, sir?"

He blanched, showing his guilt.

The plastic beads adorning the med tech's braids clicked merrily as she shook her head. "I gave her some crackers, but she should've eaten something before she took those painkillers."

"What painkillers?"

"I asked Marissa for some aspirin," Kenna said. "No big deal."

He exchanged a look with the med tech.

She shrugged.

He hoped whatever it was she'd taken kicked in soon.

"Thanks. I'll see she gets food in her stomach right away." Drake draped his arm over Kenna's shoulder. When she flinched he took perverse pleasure in pulling her closer.

Despite her protests, Kenna managed to eat a soft pretzel and drink a Coke. She glanced up from the row of Indian motorcycles she'd been admiring and froze. Impatient bikers nearly mowed her down.

He gently moved her from the flow of traffic. Her eyes were wild. Sweat trickled down her face. Oh man. He hoped she wasn't going to throw up. "What?"

"The head of my department is right over there. Omigod. That suck-up Trent is with him!" When he tried to peer over her shoulder, she clapped her palms on his cheeks, holding his head in place. "No. Don't look."

"What do you think he's doing here?"

"Weaseling his way into Dr. Herbert's good graces." She gasped. "Shit! Herbert's posing with the Hooters girls. And that cheapskate Trent is paying for it."

Kenna seemed to be missing the main point; Trent could've seen her and snatched her purse. Or paid somebody to do it.

But why? For kicks? For spite?

Drake needed to see what this Trent guy looked like. He craned his neck despite Kenna's paranoia.

The chunky, mustached, bald guy wearing black socks with sandals had to be the professor. Christ. Even his Hawaiian shorts were starched. Drake's gaze narrowed on the tall, good-looking Native American man. He had expected a greasy pencil-necked geek with a pocket protector and thick dork glasses. With the exception of the butt-length braid, Trent dressed like a frat boy: khaki Dockers, navy polo shirt, brown leather boat shoes and toothpaste white smile.

When Trent seemed to sense Drake staring at him, he frowned and glanced around.

Drake turned back to Kenna.

"They're blocking us in, we've got no way to get out of here," she said in a panicked tone. "We have to get out of here right now before they see me."

"Relax."

"I can't. Oh God. Here they come." Her slender arms snaked around his neck. Lush lips locked to his. Her tongue slid into his mouth and he fell into paradise.

While kissing the hell out of him, she not so subtly walked him backward. A motion detector beeped as they entered a tourist store directly behind them.

He'd just started to sink into the impulsive kiss when Kenna abruptly ended it and slithered from his grasp.

She snatched two T-shirts from a discount rack and race-walked to the dressing rooms at the back of the store. She zipped inside one room and wrenched the curtain closed.

Drake waited maybe thirty seconds before he followed her. He yanked the curtain open. Just as he'd suspected. She wasn't modeling the latest in biker fashions. She was hiding.

"What are you doing in here?" she hissed, jerking the black curtain back in place after he'd crowded in.

"What do you think? I'm offering an opinion on which T-shirt looks best. Though, I wish you would've grabbed a pair of those edible underwear."

"Go away. The clerk will suspect—"

"We're having a quickie? Probably. Especially after that very public knock-out kiss you gave me."

She looked down at the bulge in his jeans and blurted, "It didn't mean anything."

"Wrong."

"It was just a diversion."

"Prove it." He reached for her. Wasn't much space for her to evade him in the cubicle.

"I don't have to prove anything."

"What are you afraid of?"

Kenna stood absolutely still.

Drake angled forward, watching her eyes soften as he reconnected their desire. A brush of his mouth. Another, more momentary than the first. He swept his tongue across her lower lip, retreating a fraction of an inch so his breath drifted over the damp spot he'd created.

She licked her lips and tasted him.

"Tell me you don't want to feel my mouth on yours," he demanded.

"Drake—"

"Do you want my hands on you?"

"Drake—"

"I'll do whatever you want, Kenna. However you want it. All you have to do is say yes."

"Yes, damn you."

He grinned.

"But you don't have to be so smug about it." She slid her wet lips over his until they parted and thrust her tongue inside his mouth.

Drake groaned and hauled her closer, aligning those sweet feminine curves to his harder contours. He feasted on her. The tangy flavor of her. The way her body sought his even when she didn't realize it. Dragging his mouth up the firm line of her jaw, he whispered, "Wanting to touch you has been driving me out of my mind since I saw you in this crazy getup this morning."

Kenna shivered when he tickled the inside whorl of her ear with his tongue. "How can you make me so hot and lightheaded from a simple kiss? Especially when I don't trust you?"

"Why don't you trust me? I'm one of the good guys, remember?"

"So you say." She snorted. "The loser jerk who tried to steal my purse didn't scare me nearly as much as you do."

That comment almost jolted him out of the moment. "What?"

"Never mind. God my head hurts."

"Poor baby. You want me to rub it?"

"You think it'll help?"

"I can think of other places I'd rather rub." He traced the pulse tripping in her throat, over the generous swell of her breasts, past the tips of her hardened nipples and slid his hand under her clingy skirt. "I'll make you forget about the pain. Let me make you feel good."

"Why?" Her fingers dug into his biceps. "What's in it for you?"

"Besides the thrill of having my hands and mouth all over a totally hot biker babe?"

"Don't pull that self-righteous bullshit. In my experience men always want something in return."

"You caught me there."

"Aha. You do want something."

He paused and studied her rapt face. "Yeah. I want to make you come. I want to hear if you make that little hum of pleasure in the back of your throat like you do when I kiss you. I want to watch your face." He trailed a string of kisses back to her ear. His tongue flicked her velvety earlobe. "What's it gonna be?"

She gasped when he bit down.

"Is that a yes?"

"Yes."

"Turn around and face the mirror, hot stuff."

Drake expected her to object. Instead she twirled and settled her delectable ass against the hardness lurking behind his zipper. A tiny sigh escaped her lips as she gyrated against him.

"Lift your skirt for me, Kenna."

With deliberate provocation, she bunched the clingy fabric in her fist and slid it up her creamy thighs to reveal the black lace thong.

His cock twitched at the wanton picture she made.

Drake splayed one hand against her soft abdomen, holding her in place. The other skimmed over that scrap of lace and slipped between her legs.

Kenna's breath hitched when he pulled aside the tiny triangle and rubbed his middle finger around the soft damp heat of her sex.

She moaned. Wound her left arm above her head and tightly clasped the back of his neck.

He brought his finger up through her glistening pink folds until just the blunt tip connected with her clit. Drawing small circles over that distended flesh, he watched the pleasure play across her face. The warm female scent of her arousal caused his male instincts to insist he take her. Hard. Fast. Now. Brace her back against the wall and plunge into her.

A gasp. Her long lashes fluttered and her white teeth sank into that lower pouty lip.

"No. Don't close your eyes," he whispered against her nape. "Look at how sexy you are."

Kenna blinked. Her slumberous gaze met his in the mirror. "Don't tease. You already know one touch from you sets me on fire. Put your money where your mouth is, March. Make me feel good before someone spoils the moment."

Someone? Meaning a stranger busting in? Or either one of them regaining their sense and slamming on the brakes?

He didn't have the fortitude to deny her—or himself—the satisfaction of watching her climax.

Drake nipped the tempting slope of her shoulder and dragged his thumb across creamy wetness. Her clit flowered beneath the relentless rubbing of his thumb. "Like that?"

"No, faster," she panted.

He increased the pace.

"Harder. Please. Oh God. More."

Growling at the raw need vibrating through her, he curled his fingers over her mound, pressing his palm on the ridge of her swollen pussy. "Ride my hand. Take what you need."

She did. Pumping her hips, grinding her pelvis. "Don't stop."

"I won't. Come on, Kenna, it's right there. I can feel it."

After a few hard strokes, she arched and moaned loudly.

Drake clamped his free hand over her mouth. "Ssh, baby. When we're alone you can flat out scream, but not now."

He kept an unrelenting rhythm on her pulsing clit until the contractions started.

She bit his palm.

He held fast, staggered by the strength of her orgasm when his fingers hadn't even penetrated her. Every throbbing pulse seemed to echo in his bloodstream. His cock hardened, sweat poured down his back and he staved off his own release by clenching his butt cheeks. Finally the spasms beneath his hand slowed. Stopped.

Her eyes had closed, but he didn't care. With her cheeks flushed, her lips swollen from his hungry kisses, Kenna's face read sheer ecstasy. She slumped against him.

Drake licked a trickle of sweat from her throat, trying to find his balance. "How's your head?"

"I think the top of it blew off."

Smiling, he tugged her skirt back in place. Indulged in a leisurely journey up her curvy body, promising himself on the next go-around, he'd take his own sweet time. "We'd better go."

"Mmm. I could just curl up on the floor and take a nap." She unwrapped her arm from around his neck and lurched forward.

"Whoa," he said, catching her before her forehead cracked into the mirror.

"What's wrong with me?"

As much as his male ego would like to credit her disorientation from a mind-bending orgasm, he knew better. He tipped her face up. Her pupils were small and those beautiful lavender eyes that sparked fire were unusually vacant. "You sure the pills Marissa gave you were just aspirin?"

She paused, pressed her shaking hand to her temple. "No."

"And yet you just took them?"

"Yes. My head hurt and Marissa wanted to help. That's what friends do. Besides, she gets migraines. Probably they had codeine or something good in them. No big." Kenna snuggled against his chest, her breathing deep and slow. "I'm so tired. You're so warm, Drake. I just wanna curl up and sleep."

"You can sleep when we get back to the room."

Her head lolled back to his sternum. "Wanna sleep now. In my own bed."

Drake shook her lightly. "You've got to stay awake. We rode the bike here, remember?"

"I'm not much of a biker chick. Leave me here."

"No way." He unclipped his cell phone and dialed Geo.

"S'matter? Afraid the real cops will find me?"

He stared at her. What the hell was she babbling about? Did she have a head injury? "Real cops?"

Geo's voice boomed in his ear, "Yo, boss, what's up?"

"Where's the van?"

"Parking lot behind the Super-Value. Where are you?"

"Some T-shirt shop. Look. Something is wrong with Kenna and she's in no condition to return to the motel on the back of the bike."

"What do you want us to do?"

"Meet us at the van."

Getting Kenna out of there presented a problem. She could barely stand. She'd hate to make a scene, so no way could he carry her out of the store. People would assume she was drunk. What if they ran into that Trent guy and the head of her department?

What to do?

The ideal solution clicked and he grinned.

"Kenna."

"Go 'way."

"No. If you don't snap out of this, I'll fasten a sparkly dog collar to your neck and drag you down Main Street."

"S'okay."

Drake slapped her ass hard enough to get her attention. "Good. I've always had a Master/slave fantasy. Thanks for helping me fulfill it. *In public.*"

As expected, her eyes opened. A bit blearily, but opened nonetheless. "In your fucking dreams, pervert. Let's go."

She leaned on him pretty heavily the ten blocks it took to reach the van, but she made it.

Once her head hit the seat, she was out.

CHAPTER NINE

When they'd returned to the motel, Drake had no choice but to carry Kenna to the room. Geo had followed Bobby—who'd volunteered to ride the Harley—back to the Broken Arrow to dump the bike at the campsite.

She didn't stir as he removed her boots. He debated on whether to undress her. Wasn't a flash of conscience that stopped him. The first time he peeled off her clothes and revealed her succulent body, she'd be fully conscious and a willing participant in the process.

Drake tucked her in bed with a chaste kiss on her pale cheek.

When Bobby and Geo returned, he requested that Geo run Trent Eagle through the criminal data banks. And just for the hell of it, he added Marissa Cruz and Kenna's roommate Shawnee Good Shield to the list. Seemed mighty convenient Shawnee's boyfriend had ended up with Kenna's grant last year.

He briefed them on his meeting with the local DEA agent, Mickie Fuller. She hadn't heard any rumors about Diablo. In fact, she'd questioned the validity of Drake's source of information. Yet he couldn't ignore his gut feeling that Kenna was a link and would somehow lead him to the answers he'd been seeking on Diablo. If the private party tomorrow night didn't shed new light on this case, he'd have no choice but to drop it and head back to Miami.

Darkness fell. Activity outside the motel increased as the serious partiers took to the night. Bored, Drake lounged on his lumpy bed, drinking lukewarm Mountain Dew and clicked between ESPN and Fox Sports Net. When his stomach rumbled for the third time, he eyed the Styrofoam box holding Kenna's ham and cheese sandwich.

He hated this part of the job. Killing time in another nondescript motel room. Eating crappy take-out. Watching mindless TV. His gaze flicked to Kenna for the hundredth time, curled into a ball beneath the tacky bedspread. Oblivious to the Marlins' recent homerun. Oblivious to the red wig sliding off her head. Oblivious to his concern and his obsessive need to check her vital signs every five minutes.

There must've been a powerful sleeping aid in the pills she'd taken. She'd crashed more than six hours ago. He wondered what he'd do when she woke up. Hell, the question was: What would she do when she woke up?

Would she remember the hot, unbelievably sexy interlude in the dressing room? Or had losing her inhibitions been a reaction to the drug?

No regrets on his part. He'd been so turned on he'd nearly followed her over the edge. *Stop thinking about it.* Didn't need to spend the entire evening with his cock as hard as a baseball bat.

As if sensing his intense focus, Kenna rolled flat on her back and groaned.

Immediately Drake shot off his bed and loomed over her. His fingers longed to caress her soft cheek, sweetly creased with sleep. But he jammed his hands in his pockets away from temptation. "Hey. How are you feeling?"

"Hungry." She blinked. "What time is it?"

"Nearly ten."

"At night?" Kenna frowned. "Why am I..." She patted the wig. Flipped back the covers. "How did I get here? The last thing I remember..." Her startled gaze flew to his.

"What do you remember?"

"You barging into the dressing room and then we...I mean you made me..." Her cheeks burned cherry-red.

Drake had two choices. Let her off the hook or force her to deal with the heat between them. "Say it."

She recoiled against the headboard and shook her head. The wig plopped to the pillow.

"Then I will. I made you come, Kenna."

A beat passed. The shrinking violet disappeared. She leapt from the bed, fury in her eyes. "Did it make you feel like a big macho man that you made me lose complete control? That I was begging you?"

"Yes."

Kenna paled and he backtracked in a hurry.

"I didn't give you an orgasm because my ego needed it. I did it because you needed it." He reached for her, dropping his hand at the last second when she flinched. "It was the sexiest thing I've ever seen."

She didn't look convinced.

"You have no idea how appealing you are, do you?" he murmured. "A smart brain and a smart mouth. I'll bet none of the other gutless men you've been with have stood a chance, have they?"

"What do you mean?"

"Come on. The safe men you choose. Men who follow your rules. You might be used to calling the shots, sweetheart, but so am I." He smiled. "It bugs the shit out of you that you *liked* the element of danger. That anyone could've walked in and caught us with my hand up your skirt."

"You think you know me so well? After what?" She threw her arms in the air. "One day?"

That snotty little attitude snapped his composure. He grabbed her shoulders and got in her face. "Yes, I do know you. I know how your body reacts when I touch you. I know your scent. I know what sounds you make when you can't think of anything but how good it feels when I put my hands on you. But most of all, I know that this need between us won't go away just because you want it to."

She stared at him. "It isn't the need that I want to go away."

The stark expression in her eyes knocked the fight right out of him.

Frustrated, Drake released her. "I need some fresh air. There's a sandwich on the table. I'll be back."

The heat of the day had lingered long past sunset. He paced on the concrete sidewalk in front of their room, debating on sharing his misery and stupidity with his partners.

But he'd never been the type of guy who spilled his guts. Mostly he'd sucked up his problems. When that didn't work he sucked down large amounts of tequila. Not an option when he was on duty.

Something sharp pierced his heel. He glanced at his bare feet. Shit. He'd been so hell bent on escaping from the dismayed look on Kenna's face he'd forgotten his damn shoes. Cursing, he dug in his pocket for the room key and unlocked the door.

She sat on the end of the bed, to-go carton on her lap. The sandwich untouched. She didn't bother looking up.

Her complete posture of dejection cracked that hard part of his soul he'd toughened years ago. Survival in his day-to-day dealings with criminals demanded that no part of him remained soft.

But Kenna was soft. He didn't have to be hard, crude and arrogant with her.

Drake knelt on the carpet at her feet. "I'm sorry."

Surprised, she gazed into his eyes. Nodded.

"You need to eat. Here," he picked up the box and set it on the table. "Sit down. I'll get you a soda."

She slid into the wobbly chair. "No caffeine."

"Anything else?"

"A bag of M&Ms would go a long way in redeeming yourself."

He smiled. "Done."

After she'd wolfed the sandwich, a bag of SunChips, a package of chocolate chip cookies and the M&Ms, she climbed in the shower.

The floral scent of her shampoo wafted into the room. Drake closed his eyes, steeping himself in her fragrance. Filling his mind with images of her damp skin gliding across his.

He wanted her. Wanted to taste her, warm and soft from the shower. Wanted to run his hands over every hidden hollow as she rode him hard. His cock jerked when the water shut off.

Better to avoid temptation and finish his paperwork. He spread out his notes, plugged in his laptop and didn't acknowledge her when the bathroom door opened.

It was gonna be a long-ass night.

••

A few hours later Kenna had switched off the TV and announced she was tired.

By the way her eyes darted toward the door every few seconds, Drake knew she was lying. What did she have up her sleeve?

He played along, turned off the lamps and cracked the curtains a couple of inches, allowing the glow from the stadium lights in the parking lot to cut through the darkness. He slid the chain in place and depressed the lock on the doorknob.

Drake bid her goodnight. Smiling to himself, he crawled beneath the thin cotton sheets.

No way could Kenna get out of this room without him hearing. No doubt she'd try.

Kenna was going crazy. She had to get out of this room, just for five minutes to keep her promise to call Marissa.

Especially in light of the concerns Marissa had raised this afternoon about Agent March, his agenda and his associates. Marissa might even go to the cops if she suspected Kenna was in trouble. Kenna doubted that scenario would please Mr. DEA.

Motorcycles rumbled, doors opened and shut, bottles chinked on the sidewalk. Male shouts sounded, followed by uproarious female laughter. Squealing tires. The roar of an ignition. Horns beeping. Police sirens wailing. Southern rock blaring.

She heard it all, but the only noises she cared about were the ones inside the motel room.

Finally soft snores echoed from his bed.

Thank God he'd fallen asleep fast. She'd sneak out, use the pay phone in the parking lot and sneak back in. He'd never know the difference.

The air conditioner kicked on. Time to make her move.

Kenna eased aside the polyester bedcovers. Waited a minute and sat up slowly, careful not to squeak the mattress. Dropped her feet to the carpet. Her toes connected with her Birkenstocks and her feet glided across the familiar cork soles. Her heart thumped so loudly she was afraid Drake might hear it.

A deep snort almost rattled the windows, shelving her worries. Nervous laughter threatened and she clapped a hand over her mouth.

She stood. Tiptoed to the door. With painstaking care she kept the chain from rattling by holding it in her sweaty palm as she slowly slid the rectangular lock to the beginning of the track and out.

Whew. Halfway there.

Kenna rested her forehead against the cool metal of the doorframe, trying to quiet her ragged breathing.

But anticipation warned her not to wait. With blood roaring in her ears, she placed her hand on the doorknob. Paused. She twisted the handle until she heard a tinny click.

Yes!

She gently pulled until the door released from the frame. A tiny crack of light appeared. More light flowed into the room as she increased the gap until it was just wide enough for her to slip through.

Almost there.

Then the door slammed shut. Hard warmth covered her back as the front of her body was shoved into steel.

"Going somewhere?" Drake asked with deadly stillness.

Crap. In one fell swoop he'd not only immobilized her, but demoralized her.

No plausible lie arose so she admitted, "To use the phone."

"There's a phone by the bed."

"I-I didn't want to wake you."

His hot breath stuttered across the back of her neck. "Nice try. Where were you really going?"

"I swear I just wanted to use the pay phone. I'd planned on coming right back."

He nuzzled the bare skin along the slope of her shoulder. "Liar." The air crackled with electricity.

She shivered. Although she was the tiniest bit scared of the scope of his temper, she also knew he'd never hurt her.

"Oh Kenna," he whispered in her hair, causing goose bumps to cascade down every inch of her body. "You've been a very naughty girl."

His deep sexy voice warmed her blood, sent it pumping double-time from her tingling scalp to her curled toes. Heat flashed between her thighs and tugged upwards, past her belly to tighten her nipples into optimistic points.

"What happens to bad girls who make bad decisions?" He deliberately nestled his erection into her butt.

She bit her lip, suppressing a moan.

"They have to deal with the consequences of their actions," he answered, when she couldn't.

"Do you remember what I told you would happen if you ever tried to run from me again?"

Kenna couldn't think beyond his hot mouth teasing her skin. His rigid cock pressing into her ass. He easily destroyed every bit of her resistance.

"Answer me," he demanded between tiny bites.

"N-no, I don't remember."

"Then I'll remind you." A rough hand seductively skimmed the outside of her bare arm.

Cool metal circled her wrist, followed by a decisive click.

Oh hell, *now* she remembered.

The sneaky bastard had handcuffed her.

CHAPTER TEN

Drake spun Kenna around, layering his hard body against her soft curves, restraining her against the door. Before she sputtered a protest—as he knew she was prone to—he angled his mouth over hers and kissed her.

She fought him for about three seconds. Then she groaned, thrusting her free hand through his hair and yanking his head closer.

The sweet, spicy taste of her burst on his tongue as he took the kiss, deeper, wetter, hotter. His fingertips traced a line down her strong jaw, over the pulse throbbing in the hollow of her throat to the tops of her breasts.

Drake curled his hand under the full bottom swell, languidly stroking her nipple with his thumb. Beneath the silky fabric, the tip contracted, begging for his lips. His tongue. His teeth. The suctioning pull of his heated mouth.

Kenna arched, her tongue frantically mating with his.

His hand moved over her breast, allowing his fingers to explore. He flattened his palm over her ribcage, then down over her rounded hips. His grip increased. He imagined digging his fingers into that supremely pliant flesh as he rammed his cock in and out of her body until they were both spent. He lifted the lace edge of the camisole to touch her velvety skin. He lightly dragged a rough knuckle across her abdomen from hipbone to hipbone.

She broke the kiss with a gasp. The muscles in her belly trembled. She threw her head back until it connected with the door. "Drake," she moaned.

Drake left a trail of open-mouthed kisses down her neck, across her collarbone and shoulder. His lips brushed the magic spot in the middle that made her shudder. Made her whimper. Would make her beg. He blew a stream of air over the passion-dampened spots he'd created.

"Tell me to stop," he breathed against the maddening floral aroma perfuming her skin. "Tell me to stop right now or I won't be able to. You'll be naked before you have a chance to change your mind." He waited for her answer, tasting the dew gathered on her temple while the tips of his fingers made sweeping arcs progressively lower on her quivering belly.

"I-I—"

He traced the shell of her ear with his lips and challenged, "Tell me what you want, Kenna."

Finally, she whispered, "This. You. Punish me."

Feeling smug, he kissed her again, sucking on her tongue, grinding his hard-on into the soft notch between her thighs.

He slipped his hand inside the waistband of her pants. "Take them off," he said raggedly.

"But I've only got one free hand."

"Fine. I'll do it." Drake wrenched the fabric down until it pooled at her feet.

His engorged cock protested the pressure as he bent forward to skim his fingers from her knee up the inside of her thigh. He stopped and inhaled her fragrant juices. Oh yeah, he'd taste that sweet musk very soon. For now, Drake yanked aside the little scrap of lace that passed for underwear. Circled his middle finger around the outside of the wet slit and then up, between her folds until his fingertip unearthed that elusive bit of throbbing flesh.

Her body twitched. Her pelvis bumped closer as her lips blindly sought his.

Drake kissed her, a voracious meeting of open mouths. He changed the angle of his hand, pushed his finger into that hot, moist tunnel.

Nothing on earth compared to the first penetration of a woman's pussy. Wet. Tight. Petal soft.

He feathered his thumb across her clit as his finger plunged in and out. His tongue twined with hers. He could taste her desire. When Kenna was wetter yet, kissing him harder, he added another finger and dove deeper.

She ripped her mouth away on a gasp. "Make me come like you did before." She grabbed his head, forcing him to meet her wild gaze. "Suck on my neck." Her cuffed hand tugged him by the hair to the exact spot she craved his mouth. "God, yes. Right there."

A shudder wracked her system when he buried his lips in the graceful curve where collarbone met shoulder.

The exotic scent anointing her drove him mad. His cock poked into his stomach, leaving a wet spot as evidence of his extreme arousal.

Kenna's breathy moans escalated. Her interior muscles rippled and tried to pull his whole hand inside her slick channel. Beneath his stroking thumb, her clit pulsed. Her nails dug into the back of his hand as he gave her exactly what she wanted.

She thrashed and began to cuss like a sailor.

Drake's mouth broke into a quick grin. Then he sank his teeth into her neck and sucked hard.

Her orgasm hit.

And this time, he let her scream.

He pumped in time to the spasms, slowing down as the tremors subsided.

Kenna sighed.

"You okay?"

"Mmm. I should be bad more often. That wasn't exactly a punishment, Drake."

He eased his fingers from inside her and stepped back.

She smiled at him; sated, sexy and slightly sleepy.

Drake brought his fingers to his mouth and noisily sucked them clean.

Heat flared in her eyes, snapping her from the languid afterglow.

"That wasn't your punishment." He tugged her by the chain on the handcuffs.

"What? What else?"

"You'll see."

"Umm. Are you going to handcuff me to the bed?"

Excitement? Or fear that made her voice waver?

"No, someplace more limiting to your movements, I think."

"But I want to be able to move," she protested.

"I know. Those are the consequences for trying to run out on me." Drake led her to his rumpled bed and extracted a small key from inside the leather pouch. He flipped on the wall lamp. Soft peach light radiated from the orange shade and filled the room. He guided her into the bathroom.

"Step up on the edge of the tub."

"What are you going to do?"

"You'll see." He tapped her ass. "Come on, hop up."

She complied without arguing, which surprised him. Before she realized his intentions, Drake unlocked the handcuff from his wrist and fastened it to the shower curtain rod. He jerked hard. Didn't budge. Good and sturdy.

He turned and got a face full of satin covered breasts.

Kenna wrenched back, rattling the handcuff chain. "Omigod! You can't be serious!"

"I'm totally serious. You've still got one hand free. If you complain I'll use both cuffs on you."

She growled.

He fingered the straps of her silky camisole. How had he forgotten to remove it? He rooted around in his shaving kit until he found his pocketknife. As he snapped it open, he said, "Hold still." He wormed his hand under her top, momentarily distracted by the soft press of her breasts against his rough knuckles. He placed the dull side against her breastbone with the blade facing out.

When she flinched, he looked up into her panicked eyes.

"Relax. I'd never hurt you. I just hope this wasn't your favorite shirt." He sliced through the fabric slowly until it hung in two sections, giving him his first glimpse of her naked breasts. The knife dropped into the tub.

Jesus. Talk about a killer rack. If he didn't touch them, like right now—and then, ahh, they were in his hands, his mouth. The softest skin in the world spilled out between his spread fingers while he suckled at the pebble-hard nipples like a starving man.

Kenna's knees gave out on a whimper.

"Hold on," he said and drew her upright again. He fastened his mouth to hers, eating at those well-kissed lips, licking at the warm wet cavern of her mouth. When he pinched her nipple she arched into his palm, moaning against his lips.

Drake tipped her face back. "Look at me."

Her eyes opened. Even in the near dark they were slumberous, sexy, needy.

He curled his knuckles down her cleavage. Plumped those gorgeous globes together with greedy hands. Snaking his tongue into the crevasse, he groaned with sheer lust. "I want to feel my cock here. Watch your mouth sucking the head as I slide it up and down through this tight valley." He nipped one ruddy tip. Trailed open-mouthed kisses to the other, lapping wide circles around the pale pink areola, but never letting his tongue connect with the distended point. He softly blew a cool breath across the wetness. "Will you let me?"

"Yes!"

He chuckled, closed his mouth over the needy nub, suckling until it nearly reached the back of his throat. Then he released the warm sweet flesh an inch at a time, biting the impudent end with his sharp teeth. Then he repeated the process just as meticulously on the other breast.

"Drake, please—"

"I know baby, me too. We're getting there. But I need to impart the consequences in more detail."

She wouldn't survive.

Drake's hands, his mouth, God, his *tongue* all working together was like being zapped by continuous jolts of electricity. Her head spun, her body tingled, she was utterly at his mercy.

She loved it.

Kenna never imagined it'd be so…freeing to give up control. Okay, he'd taken control, but who was she to quibble?

"You're trembling," he said. "You cold?"

Was he kidding?

Before she could answer, his tongue dipped into her belly button. "Where's the sexy little bell you teased me with yesterday?"

"It was a fake."

"You don't have your navel pierced?" He flicked his tongue in and out. Around and around until her midsection trembled anew.

"No. I'm too chicken that it'll hurt."

"How's the arm?"

"What arm?"

She felt him smile against her abdomen. "Why, the one handcuffed to the bar."

"Oh. That arm. To tell you the truth I forgot about it."

"Good." His warm breath drifted across her pubic bone. Smooth, broad shoulders brushed the inside of her knees. "Spread your legs for me, Kenna. Now."

Even his gravelly voice was unbearably sexy. She inched her right foot toward the wall.

Rough palms glided down the outside of her legs to the tops of her feet, moved inside and gently tapped her anklebones. "Wider."

The cold porcelain stung her toes as she slid her feet further apart. Her body tensed, knowing where his skillful mouth was headed. She braced herself, but nothing prepared her for the sublime feeling of his tongue burrowing into her sex.

Kenna gasped.

"Jesus, I could come just tasting you." He licked right up the center of her. Sucked. Nibbled. "A little sweet, a little salty. Yum. I could stay here all night."

"I don't think I could stand it—OMIGOD!"

His tongue had stiffened to a hard point and nimbly flicked her clit, withdrew then flicked again.

Over and over he'd zero in on her hotspot, suck on it, tease it with his lips, then retreat to nuzzle the inside of her thighs.

Every time she was sure she'd zoom into space like a rocket, he backed off. The butterfly touches of his fingers on her stomach made her whole body shake. Everything else he was doing to her made her eyeballs roll back in her head.

"Come on, Kenna, don't hold out on me." Flattening his tongue, he slid it down and jammed it deeply inside her. Then he licked a crooked path back up.

She moaned. "If you'd stay in one place long enough—"

"Like here?" He bit her hipbone. His mouth seductively skated down another inch. "Or here?"

"Neither. Enough," she said hoarsely. "You win."

Drake's fingers dug into her ass, holding her still. "Are you going to run out on me again?"

"No."

"Good. Now, hang on tight." His thumbs spread her pussy lips wide open. He locked his mouth to her clit and sucked. And sucked. And sucked until she screamed and bucked against his mouth. The orgasm swamped her. Still, he didn't let up. The blood pulsating in her sex bloomed, spreading waves of heat throughout her body, as powerful as a nuclear blast.

Her vision swam. Her ears rang. She couldn't breathe. Her knees buckled.

Drake caught her.

Boneless and mostly incoherent, she wilted against him.

He must have unlocked the handcuffs, because the next thing she knew, both wobbly arms were wrapped around his strong neck as he effortlessly carried her to his bed.

She landed with a soft thud. Her ruined camisole fluttered to the mattress.

A frustrated curse. The bed dipped. Kenna opened her eyes even though her head was still spinning from the complete and utter detonation of her senses.

The sexual hunger on his face made everything feminine inside her ache to satisfy that tremendous male need. She dropped her gaze to his boxers, then looked him in the eyes. "I didn't plan to sleep with you."

"I know."

"What you said, about chemistry and wanting me and it having nothing to do with this case? Was that true? Or just a line to get me in the sack?"

A muscle ticked in his jaw. "I've never spoke truer words in my life."

"Okay. Take them off and come here. No strip tease this time."

Thank God.

Drake was naked with a condom in his hand before she blinked.

Plastic crinkled as he ripped the package open. His hand went to his engorged cock.

"Let me," she said.

"No. I'm gonna last about one minute the way it is." He rolled the condom down and crawled between her legs. The scent of her, flowery lotion mixed with the perfume of her arousal made his gut clench. It amazed him how delicate she was, the satiny smoothness of her slim hips under his rough-skinned hands.

Drake levered himself over her, bringing their mouths together. No sweet, slow entry; he plunged inside.

She was still wet, but tight. Her sheath hugged his cock like a dream. He pulled out, rammed back in. Harder.

When Kenna gasped in his mouth, he managed to stop moving. Sweat poured from him in an effort not to jackhammer into her. He was far beyond offering her tenderness, but she deserved better than him rutting on her like a crazed bull.

Dazed, she gazed up at him. "What?"

He nuzzled her temple with his cheek. "You are so fucking hot, Kenna."

Confusion flitted through her eyes.

Drake kissed her again. Then he began to stroke. Slow and shallow. Whatever reluctance she'd had disappeared.

Kenna arched, grabbing his ass and trying to drive him deeper.

Holy mother that felt good. But he wasn't ready for it to be over quite yet. He fought for control.

So did she, twining her arms around him, brushing those tempting breasts and beaded nipples against his chest. Biting his neck, trying her damndest to send him over the edge.

He forced her to meet his gaze. "You." He pushed inside her halfway. "Drive." Then slid out all the way. "Me." Thrust in another inch. "Fucking." Pulled out again and paused before he whispered, "Crazy," and slammed into her to the hilt.

Her hips came off the bed. She ground into him, meeting him hard thrust for hard thrust. Her breasts bounced from his driving force. Her short nails clawed his back, digging for purchase on his sweat-slick skin.

It wasn't enough. Drake needed to be deeper inside her. Breaking the pounding rhythm, he leaned back. "Put your feet on my shoulders."

She moaned, twisting her head from side to side. "God. Don't stop *now*."

"Just for a minute." He shoved two pillows under her hips, lifting her higher.

Her toes walked up his chest until her heels sank into his collarbones.

On his knees, he grabbed her around the legs and jerked her closer, the smoothly rounded globes of her butt pressed against the hair on his thighs. He didn't take the time to marvel at her luscious ass. His cock had taken over his thought processes and was intensely focused on one thing: reconnecting with that sublimely snug pussy.

In the next second it did.

Not a wet dream. He groaned. She groaned. He couldn't resist that tighter clasp. The suctioning pull of her internal muscles urging him toward bliss.

Kenna reached for his hands.

Drake held on as that familiar feeling started in his balls. Harder-faster-harder-faster; he focused on the physical sensations, only aware of the driving need to mate. The emotional stuff could come later.

Much later.

Each stroke brought him closer to that intangible pleasure point until he was finally there.

He threw back his head and roared as a swirling rainbow of light exploded behind his eyelids. His brain rattled around inside his head at the sheer power of it. Seemed his life force spurted out the end of his cock in great spasms into her moist heat.

Depleted, he stopped moving and tried to regain his balance.

But the contractions continued, rhythmic clenches squeezing his cock like wringing the juice from an orange.

He glanced down at Kenna, watching as she came in silence. White teeth digging into her well-kissed lower lip, beautiful face flushed in rapture. Small hands locked to his. One final thrust of her pelvis, she relaxed and expelled a satisfied sigh.

Drake gently settled her legs beside his on the mattress. Still fully seated inside her, he lowered his head, running his tongue across the seam of her lips until she opened her mouth to him.

Her kiss was devastating. Hot and sweet. Packed with more raw emotion than he'd expected she'd show him. Then again, so far she'd held nothing back from him, in bed or out. She seemed content to let him lay on top of her, so he did.

Truth was, he didn't know if he *could* move. He'd thought it would be good between them, but not like this. Not earth-shattering. Life-altering.

Drowsy, sated, surrounded by the reckless scents of passion, her warmth, her utter trust, a peaceful feeling settled over him, one he hadn't felt in…well, ever.

Had he really only met her yesterday?

After a time Kenna grunted. "I like that you're as solid as a rock, but I can't breathe. And I'm thirsty."

"Probably from moaning my name," he whispered in her hair.

"Cocky man. You did your share of moaning too."

"I know." He kissed her nose and slipped from her body. "I'll be right back."

Drake disposed of the condom. After she'd downed two glasses of water, he shut off the light and crawled in beside her.

Unexpectedly, she twined her sleek limbs around him.

"Comfy?" he murmured, stroking her arm.

"Mmm."

"Good." He snapped one end of the handcuff around her wrist and the other around his.

Her eyes flew open. Then tapered to points sharp enough to slice through his skin. He merely smiled.

"Just in case you get any hare-brained ideas about taking off again." He tenderly kissed her forehead and gathered her close. "Get some sleep."

CHAPTER ELEVEN

Kenna snuggled closer to the furnace, luxuriating in the heat warming her body. When her nose itched and she lifted a hand to scratch it, metal bit into her wrist.

Her eyes flew open. Wasn't a furnace keeping her roasty toasty, it was Drake.

Midnight blue eyes stared back at her. "Morning," he said, his deep voice husky, scratchy with sleep.

Memories from last night flooded back in vivid, erotic detail. Oh God. She'd let him do whatever he'd wanted to her. Twice he'd woken her up in the middle of the night. Twice she'd come screaming his name. Embarrassment stained her cheeks and she dropped her chin to her—gasp!—bare chest.

"Don't." He threaded his free hand through her hair, tilting her head up to meet his uncertain gaze. "I couldn't stand it if you had regrets." When he tentatively smoothed stray tendrils from her damp cheek, she melted.

"I've never let myself go like that."

"Then I'm glad to be the lucky recipient of that pent-up passion." He bent forward to trail soft warm kisses from her jawbone down her throat. "You were amazing," he murmured.

And right then, despite everything that had happened, or could happen, Kenna fell a little bit in love with him.

"You were pretty amazing yourself," she whispered, reveling in his silky hair drifting across her skin as he bared it inch by inch to his hungry mouth.

"How about a repeat performance?"

Red-hot anticipation roared in her blood, followed by a bout of nerves. It was one thing to indulge in wild sex under the cover of darkness and an entirely different thing to expose all of her flaws in the daylight.

She blurted, "Let me brush my teeth first."

"No." Drake lifted his head from between her breasts. His blue eyes glittered with intent. "I like waking up with the taste of you on my tongue. I like knowing my taste is still on you." He settled his lips over hers, gently coaxing her mouth open.

Kenna savored his long, slow kisses. His morning erection prodded insistently against her belly, making her squirm closer. Immediately her body softened, readying for him.

He pulled back and said roughly, "Condom."

"Not until you take off the handcuffs."

After releasing their wrists, he scrambled for a condom.

Kenna snatched it from him. "Uh-huh. My turn." She ripped open the purple package and pushed him to his side. As she rolled the condom down, her eyes drank in every impressive inch. He'd been so hot for her last night—three times!—the last go around he'd been spooned behind her—he hadn't given her the chance to explore his remarkable physique.

She whistled. "I knew you were packin', Agent March, but this big gun could intimidate a girl in the light of day." She enclosed him tightly in her fist, sliding up and down his thick, pulsing shaft. A thrill shot through her when he trembled.

"Careful. That 'gun' is liable to go off." When her fingers delved further, ruffling the crisp hair leading to his balls, he jerked her hand away with a growl and flipped her on her back.

Her legs parted as he mounted her. She smiled at the fierceness in his dark eyes. That smoldering look was for her. Feeling supremely confident, she wreathed her arms around his neck and whispered, "Slow this time."

"Very slow," he agreed.

And proved just how slow he could go.

••

While Drake took a shower, Kenna called Marissa's cell phone. She left a message on Marissa's voice mail telling her that she was fine and promised to keep in touch. She felt guilty. After all, Marissa was her friend. She debated about revealing more about where she was staying, but decided she'd better check in with Shawnee while she had the chance.

Shawnee's cell phone rang repeatedly but never kicked over to her voice mail. Strange. Because the cell reception in that part of the state was sporadic, Shawnee religiously made sure her voice mail worked so she could listen to her messages.

Every time Shawnee called, she ragged on Kenna about being the only person on the planet without a cell phone. Kenna couldn't afford the extra expense, especially when the only people who'd call her lived in her apartment complex.

When Kenna thought about it, she realized she hadn't heard from her roommate in over a week. Kenna was used to Shawnee checking in every few days. A strange feeling settled in the pit of her stomach. What if something had gone wrong at the dig? What if Shawnee had been trying to get a hold of her but couldn't?

Crap. Kenna dialed her own number and punched in the code for the answering machine. Two messages. Both from Shawnee.

"Hey, *winyan*. I hope you're not home because you're out whooping it up during the Rally." Pause for laughter. "But you're probably at the library. Just wanted to let you know I accidentally hit my cell phone with a pickaxe so you won't be able to reach me. The dig is going fine. Hotter up here than on the rez, if that's possible. Anyway, I'll call when I can. Take care. Don't do anything I wouldn't." Click.

Kenna smiled and waited for the second message.

"If you're there, Kaye, pick up." Silence. A muffled curse. "Okay. Something has come up. Something I can't explain right now. Hell I don't understand what's going on so I have to get to the bottom of it myself. If I find out that fucker Trent had anything to do with this…" Heavy sigh.

"Promise me one thing. Don't jump to any conclusions about anything you hear until I can talk to you, okay? If anyone contacts you don't believe anything they tell you. None of this is my fault. I didn't mean for any of this to happen, especially not now when we're so close. And I am going to find the answers, even if it means talking to some friends of my father…shit. Hang on." A crackling noise like she'd placed her hand over the receiver, then, "Look. Someone is coming. I've got to go. Don't freak out. I'll explain it all next time I see you, I swear."

The line went dead.

Kenna stared at the receiver. What was going on? Shawnee never panicked. About anything. And what the hell did Trent have to do with anything? Is that why Shawnee was in Sturgis yesterday?

The water shut off. She'd worry about Shawnee later. She hung up before Drake caught her and grilled her on who she was calling. Sounded like Shawnee had enough problems without adding the DEA into the mix.

Drake emerged from the bathroom naked. "It's all yours."

Kenna feigned nonchalance, keeping her gaze on the stubble coating his lean cheeks and square jaw and not on the way his cock bobbed and seemed to be beckoning her closer. "Aren't you going to shave?"

"Nah. The scruffy beard makes me look more like a badass biker." He paused, fixing his eyes on the area between her thighs. "Did I give you whisker burns last night?"

"I haven't looked."

Grinning, he strode toward her. "Allow me to check."

"No!" She scrambled off the bed, keeping the sheet as a cover. "Don't we have spy stuff to do today?"

That got his attention. He changed from hot lover to coolly professional spy guy.

The transformation reminded Kenna why she was really here; how much was at stake. As much as she'd like to stick around and see what other erotic tricks Drake had perfected, after the meeting tonight, she'd have to walk away. Or sneak away, as the case may be.

No harm, no foul, right? One-night stands were old hat for most people. So why did she feel like she'd be leaving a piece of her heart behind in this ugly hotel room?

"What's wrong?" Drake asked.

Kenna managed a smile. "Nothing. I'd better get dressed before we meet Geo and Bobby."

"You going to shower?"

She yanked the strap on her heavy duffel bag and dragged it behind her. "No. Maybe later."

"There might not be time later."

She stopped in front of him, close enough to touch him, although she didn't. "Remember how you said you liked the taste of me on you? Well, same goes. I like the smell of you all over me. I don't want to wash it off."

Kenna swept past him into the bathroom and locked the door.

Great. His dick was hard again. Drake shoved his hands through his hair, and paced, feeling agitated, edgy, antsy. And for once it had nothing to do with his job.

He had it bad. He was absolutely nuts about his informant.

Hell. He was so screwed. Frustrated, he picked up the wet towel he'd dropped and whipped it hard at the cock-eyed headboard. Didn't help.

Dwelling on it or her wouldn't change the situation. Determined to keep a professional distance, he dressed quickly and by the time Kenna surfaced from the bathroom, he'd gotten himself under control.

Drake gave her what appeared to be a cursory glance—when in his mind he devoured every detail. She'd dressed more to the personality of Kaye than Kenna today. Ankle-length loose khaki pants, a modest olive green tank top and ratty tan Birkenstocks. She hadn't bothered with make-up. It didn't matter. She still looked good enough to eat.

"Bobby and Geo are bringing back lunch," he said. "Hamburgers okay?"

She nodded.

Drake rifled through his notes, deliberately avoiding her gaze. "Are you wearing that tonight?"

He didn't see her wince.

"No. I brought another outfit." She paused, shuffled her feet. "Do you want me to change into it now?"

"Later is fine." He glanced at the alarm clock on the nightstand. "Let's go. They're waiting."

••

Later, as Drake conferred with Geo and Bobby, Kenna alternately read and dozed. She'd been unnaturally quiet all afternoon. He'd almost convinced himself her nervousness about the meeting had caused her wariness. Yet he had a sneaking suspicion he'd made a tactical error on the relationship front.

Drake snorted. What relationship? Guard and prisoner? When he had the information he needed on Diablo he'd be on a plane for Florida. Kenna knew the score and wouldn't expect anything more…would she?

He glanced at her sleeping in the chair.

"The reports you asked for came back," Geo said.

"Anything?"

"Surprisingly, yes. Got a hit on two of them. Whose do you want to hear first?"

"Read me Trent's."

Geo slid on his reading glasses. "Our buddy Trent was arrested in Ohio for unlawful discharge of a firearm within city limits a few years back."

So despite Kenna's denial, Trent could've been the one who'd shot at them. "He do any time?"

"Slap on the wrist."

"Anything else?"

"Brought in a couple of times for suspected gang activity. Released without being charged. Nothing since he moved here, except a couple of speeding tickets. His credit report is a nightmare. Guy doesn't have a pot to piss in."

Definitely a motive there. "Marissa?"

"Clean as a whistle except for a few parking violations." Geo frowned and scrolled down.

"And the girl?"

"Shawnee? Beautiful woman, at least in this picture." He passed the photo to Drake. "Doesn't she look like an Indian princess? Tiny little thing. She can't weigh more than a hundred pounds—"

"I don't want her measurements, Geo."

Geo scowled and tucked the picture back in the manila folder. "Ah sure. Anyway, that's not the interesting part. Seems the Indian princess comes from a family that has more than a moccasin in criminal activities. Her brother Santee Good Shield heads up the Warriors motorcycle club that's based out of Mission Ridge Indian Reservation, but they've got chapters on damn near every reservation in the West."

That snapped Drake to attention. "We have a file on him?"

"Evidently it's a huge file, but there was a paperwork snafu getting it to us. From the little I read, this Santee guy is an interesting cat. He's both revered and reviled on the rez. He's rumored to make a fuck-ton of money running drugs and whores, as well as the Warriors being the go-to guys for protection. The other interesting rumor is that he gives large amounts back to members of the tribe."

"Do the Warriors have a presence in Sturgis during the rally?"

Geo shook his head. "The Compadres won't let them wear their colors. They waited on the outskirts of town for the Warriors to show up and forced them to turn around. Anyway, Shawnee also has a criminal record. She'd been in and out of juvenile on the Mission Ridge Indian Reservation. Since those records are sealed I don't have a clue why she spent time in there. Then at age eighteen, she did a year in the county jail on an accessory with intent to distribute charge. She skated by without being charged a felony because she cut a deal with the Feds and testified against her co-defendant."

"You shitting me?" Kenna's roommate was a convicted drug dealer? God, did she even know about that?

"No. And it gets better. Know who Shawnee's co-defendant was?"

"Who?"

"Her father, Royal Good Shield. After she rolled on him he got twenty-five years in the state pen."

Drake whistled. "Anything since?"

"Nope. She finished college and works freelance for the BIA and the South Dakota Department of Transportation mapping Sioux burial sites." Geo tossed his glasses on the table and sighed. "But we both know how hard it is to resist going back to a normal life once they get a taste of a bigger payoff. Especially when her brother is the big bad biker dude, with a big wallet full of cash and a soft spot for his little sister."

Kenna's angry voice broke the silence. "You had no right. You had no fucking right to run your nasty little report on my friends."

Drake's head whipped in her direction. "You *knew* Shawnee had done time?"

"Yes, I knew. And one thing your slice of shit report doesn't tell you is what really happened ten years ago. And why Shawnee became a sacrificial lamb to save the rest of her family from their abusive father."

"Kenna—"

"Shawnee would never do anything to hurt me. Never. So cross her off your list. Besides, she's in Harding County on a dig. There's no way she could've shot at us."

Geo shook his head. "She's not at the site. We checked with her supervisor. No one has seen her for two days."

Kenna fidgeted and glanced at her hands.

Drake's gaze locked on her. "But you did. When did you see her last, Kenna?"

"Why does it matter?"

"Because you're making me think you're covering for her."

"I'm not covering for her. I've got no reason to. Neither of us has done anything wrong."

"Then answer the question."

"Fine. I saw her yesterday in Sturgis when you left me outside the bar."

Son of a bitch. He clenched his hands into fists. Counted to ten. "Why didn't you tell me?"

Kenna shrugged. "I didn't get a chance to talk to her before she took off."

"You don't think it's coincidence you got mugged when she was skulking around?"

"Doesn't matter. I trust Shawnee way more than I trust you so just drop it, Agent March." Her angry gaze flicked back to him. "Why didn't you just ask me about her?"

Drake leaned against the wall. "I did. You didn't say one goddamn word about her being a former dealer, Kenna."

"She's not a former dealer! She's an archeologist!"

"Explain why you didn't think her criminal record was relevant information after someone tried to kill you?"

Kenna didn't say a word.

"As for your buddy Trent, who you assured me didn't have the balls to fire a gun, well, surprise, surprise. He's been arrested for that very thing. So, I don't care if Shawnee is your roommate, best friend, or what. When she shows up she's got a lot to answer for."

"And Trent?"

He pointed his head toward the bathroom door. "Bobby's about to check that out."

"What am I supposed to do? Sit here and nap while you pick apart my life?"

"Yes."

She glared at him before sadness set in. She turned her head away and closed her eyes.

••

Kenna hadn't uttered a sound in hours. Drake and Geo worked. Bobby returned without any information on Trent's recent whereabouts. He knew better than to ask Kenna.

Drake controlled his burst of anger when Bobby told him Trent also lived in Kenna's condo complex.

Why hadn't she told him?

Because you've been a bully and she's got a reason not to trust you.

Shit. He'd fucked this up every possible way.

"Takes me awhile to get ready so I should go get started," Kenna said.

He rose to his feet. "I'll come with you."

"Not necessary."

Their gazes met. Clashed.

Defiant, she lifted her stubborn chin higher. "Relax, Agent March. I won't run out on you. I'm fully versed in the consequences." She held out her hands. "You gonna cuff me again?"

The little snot had the audacity to throw that in his face? "No."

"Then the key, please."

Drake fished the old-fashioned fob from his pocket and tossed it to her. "I'll be over in a little bit. Don't go anywhere."

"I know you don't trust me, boss. But remember the sooner you get your information the sooner I can get back to my real life." With a haughty toss of her head, she exited the room.

He sagged against the paneling, somewhat reassured to see her temper had returned.

"You stupid son-of-a-bitch. Did you have to sleep with her?" Geo demanded.

"Yes," Drake snapped, "I did."

Silence.

"Shit, Drake, this ain't no run of the mill case. You're in deep trouble with her, aren't you?"

Drake merely nodded.

Geo stared at Drake thoughtfully. "What are you going to do?"

"My goddamn job."

"But you've never messed around with an informant. You've never stepped over that professional line. What is so special about her that makes you act so—"

"Drop it. I'll deal with it—and her—later."

The toilet flushed.

Bobby stepped out of the bathroom. "Did I hear the door slam?"

"You'd better deal with it now. If your judgment is off even a little, you could be putting us all in the middle of a shitstorm."

Confused, Bobby asked, "Deal with what? What'd I miss?"

Geo sighed. "I'll tell you when you're older, kid. Let's get back to work."

••

Drake managed to stay away from Kenna for another hour. Since she'd taken his key, he was forced to ask the front desk for a spare. He'd be damned if he'd stand in front of their room, knocking like a fool in the doghouse, knowing damn well she'd refuse to open the door.

Inside the cool, dark room, he noticed the maid had come and gone. Everything appeared neat and tidy.

His eyes narrowed. Too neat and tidy. No clothes strewn on the floor. No frou-frou female toiletries spread across every horizontal surface. No big bulky purse. No duffel bag. No sign of Kenna at all.

His heart rate kicked double-time. Fury rose as he crossed the few feet to the bathroom door and pounded on it. "Kenna? You in there?"

No answer.

When he grabbed the doorknob, and twisted, he found it locked.

"Keep your pants on," she said irritably. "I'm almost done."

Relief swept through him like a calming breeze.

He rested his forehead on the doorjamb. "No hurry."

While he waited, he dug out his own clothes, jeans, T-shirt, leather vest.

He didn't hear Kenna leave the bathroom. When he turned around and saw her, he about swallowed his tongue.

Shiny red lips. Blonde wig. Blue contacts. Some tight pink leather contraption that bared her slender shoulders, showcased her tits and hugged her flat stomach. Next came a matching black leather mini-skirt, which reached mid-thigh. No stockings. Just smooth, sexy, mouth-watering skin. She'd finished the ensemble with black and pink stilettos.

"Jesus Christ," he croaked.

"You like?" She twirled, slowly.

He groaned when he saw how the skirt accentuated the curve of her tight little ass. That outfit should be illegal. If he had his way, no one would ever see her dressed like that but him.

Kenna dragged her duffel bag from the bathroom to the side of her bed. "How long before we have to leave?"

Long enough for me to bang your brains out.

Shit. Stop. It wasn't helping the already tense situation. But the greedy male section of his brain didn't give a rat's ass. It was fascinated by the thought of those cherry lips leaving red lipstick stains down the length of his cock as he thrust in and out of her delectable mouth.

"Drake?"

"Sorry." He cleared his throat. "An hour. Give or take."

She snagged the room key from the table and shoved it in the purse that never left her possession. "I'll go down to Geo and Bobby's room and let you get dressed in private."

"Kenna—"

But she'd scooted out the door before he could stop her.

He sighed and called Geo. "She's on her way. Have Bobby distract her while you tag her."

"Won't she get suspicious?"

"Not if you do it right."

Geo laughed. "If she finds out she's gonna kick your ass, boss."

Drake smirked when he thought of Kenna's eyes, dark with fury and her sharp tongue. Oh yeah. If he got caught he had plenty of ways to help her work out her anger.

"She's welcome to try."

••

Kenna's heels clicked as she stormed down the sidewalk.

Shouldn't have surprised her that Drake preferred the slutty look. He'd certainly preferred her slutty behavior last night. He'd fucked her three times. And first thing this morning.

Lord. What had she gotten herself into with this man? She stopped and rested her backside against the fake log siding, pressing her hand against her racing heart.

He'd run a criminal background check on her room-mate! No matter what he thought or his stupid report said, there was no way Shawnee would be involved in something like Diablo.

But a niggling fear arose anyway. Why had Shawnee been in downtown Sturgis? What prompted Shawnee to leave Kenna such a cryptic message on their answering machine?

Kenna would have to warn her. She quickly crossed to the pay phone, dropped in fifty cents and dialed her own number. When the answering machine kicked on, she left Shawnee a detailed message about what was going down. After she hung up, she blinked back tears. She wouldn't blame Shawnee for being pissed and moving out. And it'd be Agent March's fault.

What had happened in twelve short hours? Drake had been so unbelievably tender when he'd made love to her this morning.

But dammit, it hurt, his cool dismissal when she'd appeared in her normal clothes. As opposed to the raw hunger in his eyes when she looked like someone else.

After all they'd shared last night he still didn't trust her?

Of course he didn't.

The truth blasted her like cold water. By his own admission it hadn't been Drake March, DEA Agent in bed with her last night. But it appeared Agent March was back on duty today.

Well she had news for him. It'd been Kaye Anne doing the mattress dancing with him last night, not Kenna. If he wanted to play the split personality game, take-no-shit Kenna was more than up for the challenge.

Kenna rapped on the door. She sucked the disappointment down deep inside her soul, hoping it'd stay there so she could get through this night.

Tall, dark and handsome Geo opened the door.

God, he was so gorgeous. And sweet. And thoughtful. Why couldn't she have fallen for him instead of Drake?

She pasted on a wide smile. "Hey, sugar, we ready to blow this joint?"

"You bet. But first Bobby has something to show you."

••

Drake stalked into the room ten minutes later, foul mood darkening the air around him like a shroud.

Kenna knew he'd have no problems passing as a badass biker. Everything about him screamed danger; head to toe black clothing, long hair, angry sneer, gun, knife and handcuffs.

She tried not to think about those damn handcuffs.

Briefing done, he led them to a black van lettered with "Fred's Repair Service."

"What's this? Aren't we going to the party on the Harley?"

"No. For Geo and Bobby to do surveillance they'll need this van to get through the gates since the campground is closed to everything but commercial vehicles and motorcycle traffic."

"So we're gonna walk in?"

"Yes."

"Did you see the shoes I'm wearing?"

"Tough it up, hot stuff." He gave her a "don't-push-me" look. "I've got the bike parked at the campsite in case anyone asks how we got there."

"But—"

"Get in the van, Kenna," he growled.

She stayed silent as they made last minute adjustments to the op. With the heavy traffic it took over an hour to reach the campground and entertainment complex. Once inside the gates Drake became more uptight, if possible.

"You ready?" he asked, dropping his gun, knife, and handcuffs on the seat.

"Yep."

"Tell me again what your objective is."

"Stay out of your way, sir."

His jaw tightened. "Wrong. You're supposed to stick close and let me get the information I need."

Kenna shrugged. "Same difference."

The van bumped to a stop.

"Big difference."

Before the argument escalated, Geo interrupted. "Here's your exit point. Good luck."

After the van pulled away, Drake draped an arm over her shoulder and tugged her snugly to his side. Naturally, her body responded to the call of his.

His hand caressed her bare arm. Warm breath tickled her ear. "So we don't blow this, can you at least pretend to like me?"

Kenna flashed her teeth at him. "I'll try, but no guarantees."

CHAPTER TWELVE

They exchanged few words as they wound through the crowds of bikers.

The freaks and exhibitionists were out in full force on the sultry night. Naked women wrestling in mud. Naked women wrestling in Jell-O. Naked women wrestling in vanilla pudding. A tough man contest with huge men beating the shit out of other huge men. The announcer's minions mopped the blood off the floor of the boxing ring and the next bout began.

Next to ringside was an open-air tent where twenty bucks bought a body shot from a beautiful young topless model from a leading men's skin magazine.

Drake wondered if some of those girls were even of age.

Aromas of barbecued steak, pizza, bratwurst, tacos and buffalo burgers competed with the thick clouds of motorcycle exhaust mixed with dust and anticipation. Beer, whiskey, rum, tequila; name it and a specialty vendor sold it.

Drake kept a firm grip on Kenna even when her back stayed stiff. She didn't touch him more than was absolutely necessary. He'd like to push her and demand she tell him exactly what'd put the starch in her spine, but he had to stay focused on the job.

Hard to do when several guys standing by the Porta-potties were openly enjoying hand jobs from a couple of enterprising young women.

After skirting the vendor stands, they cut through the RV area until the big black tent loomed. Drake stopped to survey the landscape.

A separate parking area had been corded off with red velvet ropes to house the custom motorcycles. He guessed most of the vividly colored machines with custom paint jobs—gas tanks, wheels and engines—were in the 100K range. Obviously the party attendees had money. His cynical side expected little of that money had been earned though an honest day's work.

Beefy guards roamed the perimeter, armed to the teeth. He'd left his Glock in the van with Geo and Bobby, hoping to present a less threatening persona. In case something went down, he had a beeper which would signal his partners for backup. Geo was someplace nearby, snapping pictures. They might get lucky and see some familiar faces from the Florida drug world. Especially since Tito Cortez was a known associate of Hector Valero, Jerry Travis's former boss in Miami.

Kenna sighed. "Are we going in?"

"In a minute." His arm slipped from her shoulder to the enticing curve of her waist and he spun her into his arms so he could hold her. "You okay?"

It freaked him out to be staring into blue eyes instead of lavender.

"I'll be glad when this is over."

"Me too." He pulled her closer yet, lacing his fingers together at the base of her spine. Pelvis to pelvis, with her warm, sweet scent filling his lungs, his cock began to stir.

"Stick close to me, okay? I don't need to worry about you while I'm trying to do my job."

"How do you plan to get close to Cortez?"

"I've got my ways." He gave her a hard look. "I want you to steer clear of him, understand?"

"Yes, *boss*." She wriggled out of his embrace and saluted.

He briefly shut his eyes as he shoved a hand through his hair. "Kenna—"

When his eyes reopened all he saw was her very fine backside. Swishing hips and bouncing ass as her long legs ate up the distance toward the entrance.

Stop her, his male side urged.

Let her go, the cop side countered.

Shit. He caught up with her as she reached the two bouncers blocking the makeshift doorway.

One guy had to be at least six-foot-eight. Few men made Drake feel small. Defensively, he stood taller. The jerk didn't even notice him as his rapt gaze was intensely focused on Kenna's chest.

"Name, sweetheart?"

"Kenna Jones," she cooed. "I sure hope Marissa remembered to have my name put on the list."

The gorilla-sized bouncer managed to tear his lewd gaze from her breasts long enough to flip through the papers on his clipboard. He glanced up and smiled lewdly. "Yep. You're free to go in." He nodded to the other bouncer, a squat ugly man who resembled Jabba the Hut. "Just as soon as we check you for weapons."

Kenna laughed nervously. "Are you kidding?"

Gorilla-man shook his head.

She spun around. "Tell me, where exactly do you think I'm hiding a gun in this outfit?"

"Don't matter. Standard procedure."

Drake withheld a growl. That bastard was using his security position as an excuse to put his paws on Kenna. He clenched his hands into fists and seethed as the second bouncer patted the outside of her legs up to her hips. Repeated the procedure on the inside. If Drake thought Kenna's back had been straight before, it was absolutely rigid now.

"Arms out," Jabba said.

Kenna complied, holding her purse in her left hand for him to check. The squat bouncer smoothed his thick palms across her bare arms. When he reached her chest he grinned, and leisurely dragged those stubby hands down her breasts, over her belly until he reached her hips. "She's clean."

If Drake wasn't worried about blowing his cover he'd have knocked the son-of-a-bitch on his ass, regardless if the guy outweighed him by a hundred pounds.

Kenna shuddered and tidied her clothes.

She had every right to hate him for the humiliation she'd suffered. Especially in light of the fact he had no real hold over her. Turning her in to the IRS had been a bluff, as had the crack about having her busted for solicitation. He'd been damn surprised she'd fallen for it.

Man. He was such an asshole. When his damn job meant more than protecting the rights of an innocent civilian, he was no different than the criminals he was trying to catch.

Kenna sauntered toward the tent flap serving as the door.

Drake followed, only to hit a brick wall. He looked up.

"This is a private party," stated the bouncer with the wandering hands.

"I'm with her."

Jabba guy didn't budge. "Name?"

"Drake Mayhaven."

The gorilla-like bouncer with the clipboard flipped through the papers. "Nope. You ain't on here."

"Look again," Kenna said sweetly. "Marissa Cruz added him last night."

"If she did, she forgot to tell us. And if his name ain't on the list, he ain't getting in."

Drake concentrated on breathing in and out slowly, trying to cool his temper. To get this close, to put Kenna in a situation she hadn't wanted to be in, only to be denied...

Kenna scooted closer, bending over to try to read the clipboard, giving the men a clear view down her top. "Sorry, Drake. You aren't on here. You'll have to reschedule your appointment with Tito, though he won't be happy about it."

"You're here to see Mr. Cortez?" Jabba asked skeptically.

"Got in from Miami last night. First chance I've had to hook up with him."

The bouncers exchanged a look that said neither of them wanted to piss off Tito Cortez. Gorilla, keeper of the clipboard, nodded to the bruiser. "Search him."

Didn't take Bouncer Friendly nearly as long to pat down Drake as it had for him to pat down Kenna.

"He's clean," the guy proclaimed.

"Mr. Cortez is in a private area in the back by the bar. Next to the demo room."

Drake's confused look wasn't faked.

"Demo room virgin, eh?" Jabba laughed. "Don't get whiplash lookin' at everything that's goin' on." His beady eyes raked over Kenna's body. "You'll fit right in, sweetheart."

"Thanks for the tip, man." Drake tossed his arm over Kenna's shoulder and led her inside.

Kenna's skin crawled. She needed a shower in a bad way and the night had just started.

Her stomach pitched and swayed with the knowledge that while that greasy, fat jerk had been copping a feel, Drake had done nothing. Nothing.

What kind of man would stand back while some strange guy got his jollies?

She shrugged from his embrace. "I need to track down Marissa."

"I'll go with you."

When Drake reached for her elbow, it tempted her to slap his hand. Instead, she retreated further. "Don't touch me."

Something—guilt?—flashed in his eyes. "All right. But we're not splitting up."

"Whatever you say. You're the boss." She sauntered toward the swelling crowd at the back of the tent. Probably where they'd set up the bar. It was as good as place as any to start searching for Marissa.

Drake didn't touch her, but he didn't give her much space either. He stayed close enough she felt his body heat. She breathed in his unique scent, leather and soap with an underlying male musk, hating the way her heart raced. Hating how her body betrayed her by going all soft and moist. The man's pheromones were a menace.

There was no sign of Marissa at the bar. "What now?"

"We wait."

"Like I haven't done enough of that today." Kenna sighed. "What do you think goes on in the demo room?"

"I don't want to know," he said absentmindedly. His gaze continually swept the crowd. "You want something to drink?"

"Ginger ale."

He refocused on her. "That's it? Nothing in it?"

"No. I don't drink."

"But that first day…"

"I was drinking cream soda. Looks remarkably like beer, don't you think?"

"You fooled me, hot stuff."

She blushed.

"God, I love it when you do that."

"What? Fool you?"

"No. When your cheeks get flushed." Despite her warning, Drake touched her. Lightly. His knuckle skimmed the soft skin under her jawbone. "You look like that right before you come. It's sexy as hell."

Desire sucked the air from her lungs.

He saw it and smiled before he swaggered to the bar.

She watched people as she waited. How did Agent March know what constituted suspicious behavior? Did he recognize anybody?

A tap on her shoulder made her jump. She turned. Marissa had snuck up on her. "Hey. I was just looking for you."

"What a coincidence." Marissa smoothed a hank of hair from Kenna's cheek. "I like you as the blonde bombshell. I know someone else who will too."

Without Drake interfering, Kenna seized the opportunity to talk to Marissa about her options. "That's good, because I don't want to pass up other opportunities. You know I need the money."

Marissa frowned and fiddled with the Black Hills Gold cross hanging from a heavy chain around her neck. "I understand. But you've got to understand your options are limited."

"What do you mean?"

"Do you remember the Mexican guy you wouldn't even consider the first night?"

She withheld a shudder. How could she forget? Especially after Drake warned her about him.

"Well, he's got a serious thing for blondes and a serious pile of money. You're exactly his type."

"But he'll remember me from that night."

"No, he won't. Trust me. You were a brunette, remember?" Marissa beckoned Kenna forward and whispered, "I can get us double. Think about it. Half as much work for the same amount of money."

"Does he know I'm strictly an escort in the purest sense of the word?"

Marissa nodded.

"What's his name?"

"Tito Cortez. Come on. I'll introduce you."

"Introduce you to who?" Drake asked.

Marissa jumped and whirled toward him. "Don't ever sneak up on me, Mr. Mayhaven."

He just grinned and passed Kenna her drink.

She glanced at Kenna. "I thought you came alone."

"She almost did." Drake paused, sipped his beer. "Seems someone forgot to put my name on the guest list."

Marissa smacked her head and groaned. "I knew I'd forgotten something. God. I'm so sorry."

"No harm, no foul," he said. "So who are you meeting, Kenna?"

"A friend of Marissa's. Tino somebody."

"Tito," she corrected. "Tito Cortez. He was also a friend of Jerry's."

"Jerry mentioned him a couple of times. Guess Cortez is a friend of my boss, although we've never met."

"Really?" Marissa placed her hands on her hips. "Who'd you say you worked for in Miami, Mr. Mayhaven?"

Kenna held her breath. She suspected this wasn't going the way Drake had planned.

"I didn't say. I'm flattered you're so interested in my life, Ms. Cruz. I work for Jesse Vasquez. Do you know him?"

"No. Tito might, though, since he's from Miami."

"Great idea. Think you can introduce us?"

"I-I'm not sure."

Kenna started to get nervous. Tito Cortez scared Marissa?

"Don't sell yourself short. I'm sure you can convince him to talk to me." Drake stared thoughtfully at Marissa's empty hands. "Could I buy you a drink before we meet him?"

The "we" part wasn't lost on Kenna. Nor on Marissa.

"Not necessary," Marissa said abruptly with a half-smile. "Better hurry if we want to catch him before the concert starts."

As they walked past the mysterious demo room, Kenna tried to peek inside. Heavy black drapes fell from the tent ceiling to the ground, concealing it completely. Thumping bass and the pungent scent of incense drifted out when a couple exited. What had put those enormous grins on their faces?

She focused on Tito's cordoned off area. With a dove gray leather couch, two leopard print easy chairs and a plush white Sherpa area rug, it was easily nicer than her living room.

Marissa motioned her over to where Tito Cortez held court.

Although Drake hung back, Kenna felt his compelling gaze laser into the back of her neck. And with Tito's eyes undressing her, she felt like a slab of meat dangled between two hungry tigers.

Didn't male tigers fight to the death for a female? But if the way Drake had been acting today was any indication, she was on her own.

She shivered.

"Tito," Marissa said, "this is Kenna."

Kenna took his outstretched hand and yelped when he yanked her directly onto his lap.

"A screamer," he said. "I like that." One slender brown finger traced the exposed tops of her breasts. "And I definitely like these."

She wanted to snap that rude finger in half, but she played along, knowing he was the type of guy who'd enjoy it more if she fought him. Thankfully, he quickly tired of groping her and moved on.

His hand smoothed her wig. "You a natural blonde?"

"Wouldn't you like to know." Ooh. Ick. What had prompted her to say that? Taunting the tiger wasn't in her best interest.

"Not so easily swayed by my charm, eh?"

"No. Bet you don't have to work for anything. Bet you always get what you want, huh?"

"Yeah. So you wanna bounce around on my machine? It's a great big one. You'll be impressed with all the tricks I can do with it."

"I can't wait." Kenna tossed a quick glance over her shoulder. Marissa had her back to Drake while he was deep in conversation with another bodyguard. Didn't seem to be paying the slightest attention to her at all. Jerk.

She smiled—pure sugar. "Tomorrow night?"

"What about tonight?" he demanded.

She leaned forward and whispered, "A girl has to get her beauty sleep."

"You don't need it."

"What a sweet talker. I thought you were going to the concert?"

"You could come along. It'd be a kick."

"ZZ Top isn't my bag." She ran her fingertips up the front of his silky blue shirt. "Think of me tomorrow. I know I'll be thinking about you and your big bad machine."

Tito squeezed her thigh. "You'd better make it worth the wait." He frowned. "Who's that asshole talking to Marissa? He's sending you dirty looks."

"I expect he's mad I'm taking up all your time. He's waiting to talk to you."

While Tito was distracted, she slid from his lap and stood on shaky legs. "Until tomorrow."

"Yeah." He licked his lips as his eyes devoured her breasts. "Why don't you pick out something from the demo room?"

"Maybe I will. What do you like?"

"Surprise me."

As Kenna walked past Drake she refused to meet his hard gaze.

"He's all yours," she said and made a dash for the demo room before she lost her nerve.

CHAPTER THIRTEEN

Drake forced the rage from his face and the jealousy from his soul. Cortez had no right to paw Kenna. She hadn't been happy about it either, though to casual observers it might appear she'd enjoyed sitting on his lap.

He was beyond a casual observer when it came to Kenna. The woman had gotten under his skin. If this had been a normal situation, he wouldn't have let her leave the house in that sexy getup, or allowed her within a hundred feet of Tito Cortez.

Marissa tapped his arm. "I'll introduce you now, then you're on your own."

He followed her into the living room setup. Although his expression and posture remained neutral, he was strung as tight as a piano wire. He'd counted four bodyguards—all armed. Didn't sit well that he'd had to leave his Glock. Also didn't sit well that he had no idea where Kenna had run off.

"Tito, this is Drake Mayhaven. He wanted to meet you."

As they shook hands, Tito's cold black eyes never left his face. "Should I know you?"

Drake was used to paranoid drug dealers. He knew how to play the game. He sprawled in the corner of the couch and glanced around with appreciation. "Nah. I'm nobody. Great party. You throw one like this every year?"

"My cousin does. It's a business thing."

"Ahh. Business must be good."

"Can't complain. There a reason you're so interested in our business?"

"Maybe. We've got some mutual friends."

Nothing changed in Tito's hard expression. "Yeah? Who?"

"Jerry Travis for one."

"How'd you know Jerry?"

"Here and there. During Daytona he said I ought to check out Sturgis. Evidently he had a wild time last year."

"Pity he won't make a return trip."

"Got that right." Drake frowned. "Freaked out a lot of people in Miami, his untimely death."

"And some, not so much."

Drake lifted his brows. "Funny. That's exactly what Jesse Vasquez said."

From a metal tub filled with ice, Tito unearthed two Coronas. Set one on the table in front of Drake. Opened the other. Sipped. "So you know Jesse Vasquez."

Drake nodded.

"You work for him?"

"In a manner of speaking." In actuality Jesse Vasquez worked for Drake after he'd turned DEA informant five years ago.

"His wife had her baby yet?" Tito frowned. "What's his wife's name again? Caroline?"

"Carmella. And no, she's got a coupla weeks left."

Outside, an engine revved, men shouted and rocks plinked against the canvas wall. One of Cortez's bodyguards went to check it out, gun drawn.

"What's this, their fourth kid?"

"Seventh. Graciella was number four." Drake grinned. "Of course Jesse's hoping for a boy this time. After six girls the poor man is entitled."

Tito nodded. "Good thing he's got a big enough house for all those kids. I tried to buy a place like his in South Beach myself. Beautiful area."

Drake permitted a tiny frown. "Jesse's never lived in South Beach."

"I know. Didn't know if you did."

After an uncomfortable pause, Tito nudged the extra beer Drake's direction. He'd passed Tito's first little test. Adrenaline crashed through his system. This was it. Tito would either talk or dismiss him.

"Did Vasquez send you here?"

Be nice to have a bottle opener, Drake thought. He'd been lucky Cortez hadn't removed the top with his teeth, as protocol demanded he'd do the same as his host.

Drake twisted the non-twist off top until the metal ridges cut into his palm and the bottle hissed. Holding his beer in a mock toast, he drank deeply before answering. "In a roundabout way. While I'm on vacation, I'm checking sources to confirm or refute a rumor that's been floating around for the past six months."

"Half a year is a long time to wait to track down information. We both know how quickly things change in this business."

"Yeah, well, we hadn't put any stock into this particular rumor until Jerry Travis showed up dead."

Tito stretched his arm along the back of the leather couch. "What's the rumor?"

Took every bit of discipline to hide his pleasure that Tito had taken the bait. "It's about a group calling themselves Diablo." He paused, chugged. "Ever heard of them?"

"If I had, what's it to you?"

Drake held up a hand. "Hey man, I'm just doing my job."

"So you said." Tito studied Drake, his expression somewhere between belligerent and dismissive. "Why should I tell you anything, *amigo?*"

"Tell me. Don't tell me. It's your call. Actually, I don't give a shit either way." He threw a glance over his shoulder, then turned back and smirked at Tito. "The sooner I get this conversation over with, the sooner I can check out the demo room." Sweat trickled down his spine. The blasé attitude was a gamble.

"Maybe I should call Vasquez and see if you're really who you say you are, Mayhaven."

"Knock yourself out. He's probably home." Drake let his attention wander. A voluptuous brunette collected strands of beads as men flocked to take pictures of her surgically enhanced tits. A lanky Native American man quickly moved away through the crowd. His eyes narrowed. That guy had looked a lot like Trent. Shit. Was he chasing after Kenna?

Tito said, "You got his number?"

Drake returned to the business at hand. "Don't you?"

"Aren't you going to offer to call him for me on your cell phone?"

Drake snorted. "I left my damn cell phone at the campsite just so I wouldn't have to talk to him again. I'm supposed to be on vacation, remember?"

"No rest for the wicked, huh?" And just like that, Tito Cortez relaxed. "To answer your earlier question, I have heard of Diablo. From Jerry Travis. Last year."

"Anything since?"

Something flashed in his eyes but he asked casually, "No. Why?"

"Just curious. Like I said, Jerry came to Vasquez with this wild rumor that Diablo planned to muscle in on Vasquez's territory. Some crazy story about Diablo flooding areas with bad meth and then blaming it on Vasquez's unreliable distributors. Then Diablo would guarantee a cheaper, safer product to the customers and take over all venues."

Tito drained his beer and set the bottle on the table. Leaning forward, he said, "We heard the same rumor. Except in that version, our distributors were to blame. Know the strange thing?"

Drake shook his head.

"Meth is for amateurs and we ain't stupid enough to deal with it. Neither is Vasquez."

"Which is why we initially discounted the rumor," Drake said. "Same old bullshit story. You know how it goes, so-and-so is gonna break off and start his own network. He's sick of taking orders, he's got the start-up money, got the contacts up the ass and he's gonna be stinking rich, blah blah blah."

"Never happens though."

"The thing is, some weird things started happening within Vasquez's organization and it spooked him. So we're wondering if there was any truth behind Jerry's warning."

Tito paused, snagging another *cerveza*. "Tell me something. Did Vasquez ever get evidence trying to link one of his higher ups to Diablo?"

Bingo. "Why?" Drake waited through Tito's indecision on whether or not to share information.

Finally Tito said, "Fuck it. The whole fucking thing was just weird. Because my cousin Anson did. Guess who was the supposed defector?" A ghost of a smile played around Tito's mouth. "Me."

Drake didn't have to fake his surprise. "You? How the hell did you know it was Diablo?"

"A guess. In the last year they sent three different packages. One to me, one to Anson at his liquor store, another one to Anson at his repair shop. First was a picture of me with Hector Valero's right-hand man, Duey Barnes, on his yacht off the Florida Keys. The date on the photo matched the weekend I'd been in Miami, so whoever sent the pictures had done their homework. The second package, delivered two months later, contained a taped phone conversation I'd supposedly had with Duey about moving some money we'd 'liberated' to an account in the Caymans. Again, the dates matched. The voice on the tape sounded like mine and coordinated with the dates I'd been in Denver."

"And the third?"

"About six months ago Anson received a copy of a rental contract for a warehouse in goat-fuck Kansas. Paid a year in advance with my signature on the lease."

Drake whistled. "Your cousin didn't get suspicious?"

"At first I thought he was playing a joke, especially when I showed him the cheesy-ass picture of me and that fucking weasel, Duey. But Anson didn't know nothin' about it. Laughed our asses off, figurin' if someone had gone to all the trouble to superimpose me in a picture with Duey, they'd probably contact me for some cash to keep quiet about my secret 'connection'. Anson and I waited, wondering who the hell would be that stupid."

No shit. Who had big enough balls to tangle with the Compadres?

"Who delivered the packages?"

"The second time, Anson got the package. No threats, just the tape and a letter inside suggesting he pay more attention to my activities."

"The last time, with the rental agreement, we hired an investigator to find the start of the paper trail, but she didn't have any luck. And we never could find the courier who delivered the packages, either. Although we're assuming it was a local."

The three packages were news to Drake. "What's happened since?"

"*Nada*." Tito sucked down his beer. "Business as usual in Compadres territory. What's going on the Vasquez end? Still have weird shit going on?"

"Just Jerry's execution. We're wondering who ordered it."

"Not us."

"Then who?"

"Easy. Hector Valero."

"Jerry's boss? You sure on that?" They were getting into conjecture here, but Drake couldn't resist taking a peek into the criminal mind. Tito Cortez was a lot shrewder than he'd first imagined and a lot more dangerous.

Fury briefly distorted his vision when he thought about this lowlife putting his dirty hands on Kenna. If Cortez ever touched Kenna again, he'd break every one of his fingers, job or no job.

"No. But my theory is Jerry Travis made up Diablo to cause problems. He'd never been the most reliable source anyway. I'd bet part of what he'd been telling us was true. Maybe *he* was looking to start his own operation by causing dissention among the big players. When Valero caught wind of it, he took care of him before Jerry became a bigger problem for everyone."

"That does make sense. I'll pass it on."

"Good." Tito glanced at his Rolex and stood. With obvious pride he made a big show of adjusting his cut—his leather vest—and the patches all over it told of his past with the club and his place in it. From what Drake could see, Tito was top tier. "Tell Vasquez I'll be in touch."

"Will do. Thanks for the info. Now I can really enjoy my vacation."

Tito departed without a backward glance.

Drake took a minute to collect his thoughts. So far, it sounded like Diablo had a personal vendetta against the Compadres, and Tito Cortez in particular. He felt like he was running in circles. Maybe Tito was right. Had this whole thing begun (and ended) with Jerry? Had Jerry been purposely feeding the DEA bogus information? Who had delivered the three mysterious packages? And why?

Hell. He was no closer to finding answers than he'd been for the last two weeks. As soon as he reported the lack of information to his supervisor, she'd advise him to drop it and return home.

Like he didn't have fifteen cases waiting for him in Miami. He wouldn't get a moment's peace. He probably wouldn't get a decent night's sleep for the next six months. When he'd slept last night, he'd slept well.

His thoughts drifted to Kenna. She'd taken off the minute Cortez had released her, not that Drake blamed her, but where had she gone?

He looked around. Marissa had caught Cortez on the way out. His eyes narrowed as Cortez peeled off some bills from a wad of cash in his pocket and handed them over.

Their eyes met. Drake stalked toward her. "Where's Kenna?"

"What do you care? You got what you wanted from her."

He doubted Kenna had told Marissa about last night, so he played dumb. "What do you mean?"

"Your meeting with Cortez, which is all you were really after from her anyway. Happy now?"

His temper flared. "You have no idea what you're talking about."

"Yes, I do." She flipped her hair over her shoulder. "She's *my* friend, Mayhaven. I know her a lot better than you do."

"Some friend," he sneered back, "selling her *tour guide* expertise to the highest bidder, which is beyond fucking ridiculous. What's your cut?"

Marissa fumed.

"Just tell me where she is."

"You know, I don't think I will. I don't like you and I don't trust you. Besides, since you seem to think you're so damn clever, figure it out yourself."

Marissa disappeared into the masses like smoke.

Kenna had probably high-tailed it to the rendezvous point. He scanned the immediate vicinity just in case and his gaze landed on the curtained off area.

What the hell was the demo room about, anyway? Despite his wariness, he'd better take a quick spin inside so he could detail it in his report.

At his hard look, the bouncer moved aside without arguing.

Just inside the door, he went utterly still.

Surely Kenna hadn't gone in there alone?

••

Kenna wanted to punch any man who assumed because she'd dressed provocatively they had every right to touch her. No wonder she normally hid her body under baggy clothes. Invisibility was much safer.

She managed a tight smile for the bouncer guarding the door to the demo room. Surely he wouldn't frisk her too? He merely nodded as she ducked under the heavy swag and stepped inside.

The sweet scent of pot smoke lingered in the humid air. For a second Kenna worried the secretive demo room was a place to try different types of drugs—until she caught sight of a skinny woman on her knees, noisily sucking a big burly biker's cock.

The man groaned, grabbed the woman's head and began plunging in and out of her mouth with unrestrained gusto. With his pants around his knees, the chains holding his wallet and knife jingled with every hard thrust.

Kenna froze, unable to tear her gaze away as the man groaned and raced to the finish as the woman sucked and swallowed and made happy sounding moans.

Much as she hated to admit it, a tiny kernel of heat settled in her core. She forced herself to move forward.

Five feet away from the blowjob couple, a man sat on a hard-backed chair with a naked woman straddled across his thighs. Her long brown hair teased the crack of her tiny butt as she threw her head back in ecstasy. She lifted and lowered, using her silver stiletto heels on the chair rungs beneath the seat for leverage as she impaled herself on his cock.

The man grinned and squirted a gel-like substance—from a penis- shaped bottle no less—on her nipples. Taking her enormous breasts in his hands, he squeezed the globes together, dragged his tongue across the tops. When she moaned, he sucked, licked and bit her nipples as she began to ride him harder.

Fascinated, Kenna wasn't able to scurry away so quickly this time. As the couple climaxed—together naturally—the crowd applauded. Surprised her they didn't get up and take a bow.

Still, what would it be like to be that uninhibited? Her thoughts zoomed back to last night with Drake. She hadn't exactly been Miss Prim and Proper.

A young guy wearing a pinstriped, double-breasted suit stepped in front of the couple. "For those of you who've just joined us, Dante and Cheyenne have generously demonstrated our product Cold Heat." He held up the bottle. "Icy cold when first placed on the skin. As friction is applied, it warms, creating a delicious contrast. It's available in cinnamon and mint flavors at the sales counter at the back of the tent."

People began milling to the next demonstration. She hung back, her eyes frantically searching for the exit.

God. She felt like *Alice in Wonderland* meets John Holmes in *Wonderland:* She'd walked into the world's largest porn movie.

"First time here?" an amused male asked.

Kenna spun around and backed up, tripping in the heels. The professionally dressed guy hawking the Cold Heat grabbed her elbow, keeping her from falling on her ass.

He smiled. "Relax. I'm JJ Jameson, head of PR for Joysticks."

"What exactly is this place?"

"A place for consenting adults to see a demonstration of Joysticks' latest toys and newest products. Any other questions?"

After a slight hesitation she blurted, "Are the couples doing the presentations...umm..." *Real mature, stuttering and stammering.*

JJ lifted a dark brow. "Professionals? No. Just enthusiastic customers with a streak of exhibitionism. Why, are you interested in doing a demonstration?"

Kenna blushed.

"I'm kidding. When you make your way to the back, check out the selection of vibrators. And in the bondage garden we've got a helluva sale on paddles."

She frowned. "For boating?"

"No. For spanking."

Wow. People really did that? She knew Drake would never hit her and it'd be a cold day in hell before he let her have control. A snort escaped before she stopped it.

"Don't knock it 'til you've tried it," JJ warned.

"No judgment from me. It's just the guy I'm with, well, he's pretty dominant. Not in a bad way." Shoving aside her embarrassment, she asked, "So if I wanted to show him my dominant side what product would you suggest?"

JJ grinned. "This." He jiggled a small, sealed bottle of Cold Heat. "Guaranteed to drive even the most controlling man out of his mind."

"Where can I buy it?"

He took her hand, placed the bottle in her palm and gently curled her fingers around it. "On the house. Enjoy." With a mock bow, he departed to hock more wares.

Kenna scoped the place out and decided since she was here, she might as well enjoy herself. Maybe enjoy was the wrong word. Not shrink like a prude and run for the nearest exit.

With determination, she marched up to the next presentation and learned way more than she'd ever wanted to know about vibrators. Big thick ones. Long skinny ones. Glass ones. Smooth ones shaped like animals. Some tiny enough to wear on a single finger. Remote control models. The enormous one with ridges and bumps looked too much like studded snow tires and quite frankly, scared the crap out of her. But the ones with the clit vibration attachment had intriguing possibilities. And the woman demonstrating seemed to prefer that model, if her moans of satisfaction were any indication of quality.

As she wandered, she noticed she wasn't the only spectator unbelievably turned on. Several couples had taken matters into their own hands and were going at it right on the canvas floor. Missionary style. Doggy style. Sixty-nine. Threesomes in every combination. Moans, groans, grunts, sighs of completion. Aromas of heat and sex filled the sweltering air. She breathed deeply, letting it wash through her like a sultry breeze.

Kenna clenched her thighs together. Her sex throbbed in time to the bass thumping from the loudspeakers. Beneath her top, her nipples contracted. Her skin tingled. She wished for relief from the hot sexual ache invading her body. Staying in here another moment surrounded by people wallowing in hedonistic pleasure when she couldn't wasn't fair.

Dammit, she wanted, she *deserved* that same mindless, passionate connection. But she didn't want to join in and trust her body to a stranger. She wanted Drake.

Now that he'd gotten his meeting with Tito Cortez and had the information he needed, would he let her go?

Yes.

Kenna still wanted him, just one more time. She wanted more of the delicious heat that exploded when they were within five feet of each other.

Yet, her pride didn't *want* to want Drake. And realistically she knew he didn't want her. The real her. Kaye Anne. It'd be best to make a clean break. Grab her stuff from the motel and forget the last two days had ever happened.

Tossing the bottle in her purse, she ducked out the side exit and practically ran to their prearranged rendezvous point.

Chapter Fourteen

The night air didn't cool the warmth in her body or her rising temper.

As she picked her way back to the campsite where she and Drake were meeting, she heard the roar of the crowd and the deafening thunder of thousands of motorcycles as ZZ Top took the stage. Guitar riffs wailed and people hustled past her to catch the show.

The campground was mostly deserted now, as it was the prime time for partying. She fought her nerves, as it wasn't the smartest move wandering through the area alone. Should she have waited for Drake outside the party tent?

No. He'd shown he didn't give a crap about whether or not men pawed at her. She didn't need his brand of protection anyway.

Still, it paid to be alert. She focused her attention on the uneven terrain and piles of paper, cans and bottles littering the landscape. It'd be her luck to break her damn ankle traipsing through this cow pasture, especially since there weren't lights out this far.

Kenna had just spied the tent with a white flag and motorcycle when a big hand clamped on her shoulder. Furious that anyone else dared to touch her, she spun and let her fist connect with something solid. Blindly, she swung again, lower. Another direct hit. She'd fight; no other man would put his hands on her without her permission tonight.

She aimed higher, hoping for a headshot, but this time the blow was blocked and her attacker latched onto her wrist.

"Jesus, you little hellcat. Would you knock it off?"

She froze. "Drake?"

"Who the hell else were you expecting?"

She wrenched her wrist from his grasp. "After the night I've had you think I'm gonna take any chances?"

He stepped closer, rubbing his jaw. "I wouldn't have let anything happen to you."

Anger rose and she punched him in the arm hard enough he felt it and hard enough her knuckles smarted.

Anger sparked in his eyes. "Don't hit me again."

"Or you'll what?" she taunted. "Hit me back?"

"For christsake no. What kind of man do you think I am?"

Kenna retreated, willing her heart to drop back into a normal rhythm. "You aren't the man I thought you were, that's for damn sure."

Drake loomed over her. "What are you talking about?"

"You know *exactly* what I'm talking about." Sick of being pushed around, she pushed back. Didn't even faze him. Which kicked her resentment up another notch.

"Yeah, you're some great guy, some great protector, Agent March, letting those asshole bouncers feel me up, while you watched and did nothing."

A muscle ticked in his jaw but he stayed dangerously silent.

"And then, when you'd repeatedly warned me about staying away from Tito Cortez, when that bastard pulled me onto his lap, you stood back there like a statue and did nothing again."

Her lungs strained under the effort of her rapid, angry breaths, but she forced the cruel words out anyway. "You probably got off on it, you perv, since highhanded is your style."

"That's enough."

"I'll say. Call Bobby and Geo. I want to go home." Truer words had never been spoken. All she wanted was to crawl into her cool sheets in her tiny little apartment, jerk her grandmother's wedding ring quilt over her head and pretend the last two days were a bad dream. She clenched her jaw and blinked back the tears of humiliation and frustration burning her eyes.

"No."

Kenna's head whipped up. She swallowed hard at the raw fury darkening his face.

"You finished?" he asked coolly. "Because I've got something to say."

She managed a slight nod before she looked away. God. She really didn't want to hear his excuses.

"As an agent I've been doing this long enough that I know how to react when situations get out of control. I have to be adaptable, Kenna. I have to stay levelheaded at all times, especially when the unexpected happens. About ninety percent of the time ops don't play out the way we've planned. My job is to assess the situation and salvage whatever part of it I can without compromising my position."

Wasn't your position that was compromised, she thought mulishly.

"But when that greasy bouncer put his hands on you…"

Her gaze snapped back to his.

"As a man, I wanted to rip his fucking arms from the sockets. But instead I had to stand there and pretend I didn't give a shit. I had to stand there and watch him enjoy humiliating you." His bitter laugh cut through the night air. "Oh, and to make my night complete, I had to pretend it didn't bother me that a slimeball like Tito Cortez touched you like he had every right to."

"Drake—"

"Let me finish." He shoved a hand through his hair. "I've had to make some tough decisions, but I've always felt they were the right ones at the time. Tonight is no exception. I had no choice. I know you don't understand. I know you're hurt that I didn't do a damn thing to stop those bastards."

Frustration sent him pacing. Finally he stopped, threw his hands in the air and said, "Fuck! I'm sorry, okay? It's my job and it sucks but if I had to do it over again, I'd probably do the same thing. And I have to live with that unpleasant fact about myself every goddamn day. I also have to live with the haunted look in your eyes and know that my decision put it there."

Kenna couldn't speak she was so stunned. It wasn't that Drake didn't have a protective streak; it just didn't matter as much as his pursuit of justice. The anguish in his eyes was real. Why did she have the urge to go to him, wrap her arms around him and murmur reassuring words when *she* was the one who'd been hurt?

Because he was hurting too. Despite everything he'd done, everything he was, she'd fallen for him.

Oh shit. She'd never been in worse trouble in her life and it had nothing to do with the IRS, the local cops, her academic standing or the low balance in her checking account.

Her heart started racing like a jackrabbit caught in a snare. And just like that scared little rabbit, she turned and ran.

Of course, Drake, being predatory in nature, only let her get about ten feet before he cornered her. He wrapped his arm around her middle, bringing her body flush with his.

Softness met hardness.

She withheld a moan as lust slammed into her like a rockslide.

His chin dug into the place where neck met shoulder and his deep voice reverberated in her ear. "Remember what happened the last time you ran from me?" He set his teeth on the tender skin of her nape, knowing it'd drive her wild.

Chills started in that sensitive spot and spread. She moaned, automatically pressing her backside into him.

Drake flipped her around. Locked her so tightly against his body she couldn't breathe. Took her mouth in a kiss so hot and needy she wondered why she hadn't crumbled into ashes from the heat of it.

Her knees went weak. She clung to him even as she undulated against the hard bulge in his jeans.

"Oh yeah. I want that wild woman who was in my bed last night."

He doesn't want the real you, her subconscious whispered, *he wants the illusion.*

Reality intruded. Outraged at the traitorous rush of moisture between her legs, Kenna bit him.

He reared back. "Why'd you do that?"

"Because I just remembered I fucking hate you."

Drake's dark expression softened. His hand shook as he lifted it to trace wispy touches along her jaw. "No, you've got that backwards. You'd hate it if I didn't fuck you."

She stared at him, at a loss because she knew he was completely right.

"This thing between us scares me too. And not just because someone was shooting at us. Or because you were mugged."

The uncertainty in his eyes sealed her fate. She wanted him. His powerful body reminded her of the spontaneous heat generated between them. She could deny them the pleasure or enjoy it.

Not a difficult decision.

Maybe she had an exhibitionist streak after all because she didn't care about anything beyond being with Drake.

"I'd forgotten you were the kiss and make up type. Okay. Let's do it. Right here, right now."

"Are you serious? Right here?"

"You got a better idea?"

"Hell yes." He grabbed her hand and made a mad dash for the backside of the campsite. Miscellaneous broken motorcycle parts were strewn across the grease-stained tarp beside the tent, giving the appearance the spot was occupied.

Kenna stopped. "What are we doing here?"

"You'll see." He led her toward the low-slung motorcycle behind the tent, kicking aside empty beer cans. "Climb on."

"Why? We going for a ride?"

Drake faced her. "The only thing I'm gonna ride, Kenna, is you."

Every cell in Kenna's body revved into high gear.

Before she asked another question, his mouth came down on hers. He ate at her lips, suckled her tongue and peeled the halter down to her hips.

Strong fingers pinched her nipples, rolling, tugging the tips until it felt like he'd unearthed a secret electric link between her breasts and her pussy.

Kenna traced the delineated lines of his abdomen, reaching past the waistband to his belt. A quick tug and the buckle gave way. Another yank and the buttons popped. Her fingers met coarse hair, then the solid reality of him. Her palm brushed the plump head, spreading the moisture seeping from the tip down the length.

He sucked in a harsh breath through his nose and kissed her harder.

His cock twitched as she alternated featherlight touches with firm strokes. She dropped kisses on the shadow beneath his chin and murmured, "You smell good."

"Ah. Christ that feels good." He widened his stance.

The almost delicate skin surrounding such pure male hardness amazed her. Oh yeah. He was definitely hot, hard and ready. Her tongue traced the seam of his lips until they parted. She left him like that, his mouth hanging open as she hiked up her skirt and dropped to her knees.

Without preamble she opened her mouth and swallowed him.

Some incoherent sentence burst from him.

Kenna sucked his cock. Her hands caressed his balls. She kept her eyes locked on his while deep-throating him.

"No," he sputtered, jerking her to her feet and hauling her into his arms.

She hid her face against his broad chest. Why was his heart racing and his breathing uneven if he hated it so much? "Sorry, I thought you'd like it."

Drake tipped her chin up. "I loved it. You can do it later, as much as you want for as long as you want. But when it happens, I want to look in *your* eyes, not colored contacts. When I'm ready to explode from the mind blowing sensation of that wanton mouth taking all of me deep, I'll be grasping your hair, not a damn wig."

His words were a balm to her soul.

"The first time I come with you tonight won't be in your mouth, Kenna."

Her own mouth dropped open in shock.

He took advantage of her lapse in concentration and quickly kissed her. His soft hair tickled her collarbone as he angled his head closer. "Let me taste you. Lift your skirt."

"Drake—" The words died when he dropped to his knees. Callused fingertips yanked aside the flimsy barrier of her underwear. Then his mouth was on her, nibbling her clit, licking the juices from her wet folds. Swirling his tongue in figure eights. Jamming it high inside her until she started to shake and whimper.

His tongue made another thorough pass from where she was soaked and aching to that forbidden area no man had breached. Little expert flicks of the stiffened tip of his wet tongue on that spot made her clench her thighs and everything else.

After one final decisive lick, he stood.

"God. I want you naked. But I need you, like now, so this'll have to do." Drake clamped his strong hands around her hips and lifted her.

After a surprised shriek, she tried to wrap her legs around his waist to catch her balance.

"Tempting. But those killer legs are gonna be hugging the motorcycle this time, not me."

"Yeah? Where are you going to be?"

"Right behind you."

Drake set her on the bike and faced her forward. The night-cooled leather seat stung her bare skin and the shock sent a current straight up her center, from her belly to her breasts to the top of her scalp.

"Put your feet on the back pegs."

Kenna glanced down in confusion. She saw the six-inch metal bars that stuck out on either side of the bike. She wiggled her foot until the middle of her high-heeled shoe was firm against the rungs. Looking up at Drake for approval, her breath caught.

Jeans undone, muscular arms crossed over his chest, hair mussed, eyes dark and needy, he resembled some pagan god, waiting for his due. Waiting for her to surrender to his every whim.

She shivered in anticipation and prepared to give in.

His hand meandered up her arm. "Grab the handlebars, hot stuff."

Kenna had to stand on the pegs to reach the chrome ends of the chopper-style grips, forcing her ass up in the air. Her nipples briefly brushed the cold metal gas tank, puckering them into aching points.

"Beautiful," he said thickly. "Don't move."

She watched as he took a condom out of his back pocket, ripped it open and rolled it down. He straddled the bike behind her. With his long legs and the low angle of the seat, he had no problem keeping his boots on the ground.

He traced the thin line of the black thong and groaned, "Goddamn you have the best ass on the planet. I'd like to take you here too." He wiggled closer, sending the bike swaying from side to side. "I want what you've never given another man."

She looked at him over her shoulder. Their fiery gazes met across her body, nothing mattered besides putting out the inferno raging inside her.

"Stop the running commentary and fuck me," she said.

Those sinful lips curled in a carnal grin. He scooted back on the bike and pressed on her lower pelvis until the back of her legs chafed against denim. The head of his cock circled her opening, spreading the wetness.

Drake slid in an inch at a time, then halfway, then he slammed all the way to the hilt.

Kenna cried out from the rush of the ultimate hedonism—her lover so hot for her he'd do anything to ensure her ultimate satisfaction. She didn't care if the whole damn campground came running to see who was making the racket.

In. It. *Out.* Felt. *In.* So. *Out.* Fucking. In. Good. Out. She rocked her hips back, meeting each forceful thrust, wanting, needing more.

"Stop. Too fast." He pushed back inside her slowly. In this position, the entire length from tip to thick root ground against the inside wall, making her gasp at the decadent pleasure. The wet sucking sounds of their lovemaking bounced off the tent and ricocheted back to them as an erotic echo.

"Right there. Harder, God, don't stop," she said on a long rush of air.

"You are so tight and wet. You feel so fucking perfect. I'll never get enough of you. Of this." He plowed into her so hard she swore she felt the tip of his cock in her throat.

Deep, fast strokes sent her breasts swaying and tingles sizzling across her skin. A soft breeze drifted across her face and she lifted her head to cool the sweat from her brow.

The fingers on his left hand dug into her hip, holding her in place as he took her as hard and fast as he wanted. He released his right hand to feather his fingertips across her right butt cheek. The rough pad of his thumb slowly traced the crack of her ass down to where his cock pumped in and out. He swirled it in her juices and then slid it back up to brush against her rear opening.

Her breath caught at the foreign sensation, remembering how sinfully good it felt when his tongue had ventured there. But she automatically stiffened up.

"Don't pretend you don't like this, you don't want this. I'll give you a little preview, hot stuff, of what I'd like to do to you. This will blow your mind."

A rush of heat flashed from head to toe. How did this man tap into the secret dark desires she'd been afraid to explore?

He drew circles with her wetness around the sensitive knot of nerves. With each pass, that wicked thumb probed a little more. Then his hand shifted and he pushed a thick finger past the tight ring completely.

"Omigod." She closed her eyes to savor the full feeling and the absolute mastery this man had over her body.

Using gentle, shallow strokes, he pumped his finger, and his balls slapped against her throbbing pussy with every delectably strong thrust of his pelvis.

The mingled scents of sex, dust and motorcycle grease surrounded them, the ultimate aphrodisiac.

"Sweet Jesus," he growled, pistoning faster and faster. His hips pounded until a satisfied grunt burst forth from him.

Kenna clamped down with her interior muscles as Drake started to come violently. Then she did something she'd never done with another lover; she dropped her hand to her clit and rubbed her clit vigorously while he pulsed and plunged and throbbed inside every part of her.

The combination sent her rocketing to an orgasm so intense she stopped breathing and her vision went dim.

Vaguely, after the white flash behind her eyes cleared and the pulsating in her lower body dwindled, she felt drops of Drake's sweat dripping on her back. Her toes were cramped and her legs shook like she'd run a marathon. Not only that, her boobs were smashed against the gas tank and her not-so-small ass was hiked up and bared to the world. Instead of instant mortification, she felt…well and truly fucked.

His satisfied sigh wrapped around her heart.

Normally she hated making love from behind, but there wasn't anything normal about the way Drake March made love. Kenna had the urge to howl her pleasure like a well-sated bitch.

Drake kissed his way up her spine. He gently bit her shoulder. His hot, stuttered breath flowed across her damp nape as a lover's caress. Leisurely, he withdrew from her body and whispered, "And to think before this I never understood the appeal of owning a motorcycle."

Kenna snickered. She nuzzled her cheekbone to the side of his face, her breath tickled his lips. "Does that make us official members of the…what is the equivalent of the 'mile high club'?" She snickered again. "The 'low riders' club?"

"Mmm," he mumbled against the tempting hollow below her ear. "Maybe it should be the 'easy riders club'?"

Her breath hitched when he sunk his teeth into that bit of salty flesh near her throat, just feminine enough to stir his dick again.

"Nothing 'easy' about the way you rode me, Drake."

His wandering mouth stilled. With the way she'd screamed and thrashed, and bucked against him, he'd assumed she'd loved it hard and rough. Loved pushing her limits. Maybe not. "Did I hurt you?"

"No."

He paused. "Good. I sense a 'but' coming."

She attempted to pull away. He held fast. "This was spectacular, but aren't Geo and Bobby waiting for us?" With awkward, stiff movements, she jerked at the pink and black lace contraption bunched around her middle.

While ordering his thoughts, Drake gently tugged at the back of the garment, helping her set it right. "Are you worried what they might think?"

"Yes. No. I don't know. I'm more worried that I'm developing a split personality. One minute you're threatening me and the next I'm letting you bang my brains out. You probably always do stuff like this."

Calm man. Stay calm. "You think this is a normal day at the office for me? That I screw every woman who crosses my path in a case?"

She scooted off the bike. "You had condoms in your pocket! What am I supposed to think?"

Breathe. Don't yell. "You sure didn't mind I stuffed those rubbers in my pocket about five minutes ago." He threw his leg over the seat and stood beside her.

"You conceited jerk!"

"Look. I grabbed them from the freebie table in the demo room, all right? I didn't come here tonight planning to fuck you on the back of a motorcycle." He rested his forehead to hers. "I don't blame you for getting freaked out. But you've got to know I've never done anything like this before."

Surprisingly Kenna didn't squirm away. "Like what? Showing me your prowess in the 'low riders' club? Or getting involved with an informant?"

"Both."

She leaned back and looked up at him, her expression not skeptical, just curious. "Really?"

"Really. I'm all about the job, Kenna. I might bend the rules from time to time, but I don't break them because that wouldn't make me any different from the guys I'm trying to catch." He had to touch her to ground himself for the remainder of this strange admission. One hand framed her face; the other skated down her smooth arm, to thread their fingers together. Amazing how perfectly they fit in so many ways. "I'm sure you've realized I'm not some smooth talkin' ladies man that has lines and lies for every occasion."

"You talked me out of my panties quick enough."

Drake grinned. "Good point. You're the exception, not the rule."

"I'm glad to hear that."

He held her and she let him. The strains of "Under Pressure" drifted on the night breeze. He wanted to be long gone by the time the concert ended and the traffic nightmare started.

"I'll signal Bobby and Geo that we're ready to go."

"Then are you taking me home?"

"Do you want to go home?"

She didn't answer.

He was so bad at this stuff. His heart skipped a beat when he asked her softly, "Stay with me tonight?"

"Because I'm in danger and people were shooting at me?"

"I think you're in the clear now." He paused, bracing himself for her rejection. "I want you to stay with me out of pure selfishness. I'd like to make love to you again," *before I have to leave you.*

"Hmm. Guess that depends. Are you going to handcuff me?"

"No."

"Can I handcuff you?"

Drake shivered at the thought of Kenna having that much power over him. She already had enough.

She laughed. "Okay. No cuffs. But you aren't the only one who picked up a little something in the demo room."

When she refused to tell him exactly what she'd bought, he shivered again. The unknown was almost worse.

Maybe he ought to reconsider the cuffs.

CHAPTER FIFTEEN

Geo and Drake conversed in low tones in the front seats while Kenna stayed in the back with Bobby. She was grateful Bobby paid little attention to her as he meticulously packed his equipment.

She needed time to sort through the emotions that were as tangled and tenuous as the slim black wires in Bobby's hands. Eyes squeezed shut, she slumped into the cushioned seat. Her mind wandered, her fingers fiddled with the straps on her purse.

How had she fallen so hard in such a short amount of time? She, polite, practical, levelheaded Kaye? Drake was so not her type. Rude. Demanding. Hotheaded. When she dated—which wasn't often—she preferred men with an academic background. Civilized men. Men who didn't raise their voices to her. Men whose idea of taking a chance was drinking merlot with chicken instead of chardonnay. Men who would never dream of handcuffing her to a shower bar and making her scream with raw pleasure.

No wonder she'd been bored out of her skull.

With Drake's hot, hard, made-to-please-a-woman body plastered to hers, it was hard to form a coherent thought, let alone an intellectual one.

But brains weren't necessarily superior to brawn—nor were they mutually exclusive, as she'd previously thought. Drake was as cunning as he was sexy. As dangerous as he was mysterious.

Just when she thought she had him figured out he threw her for a loop.

A shiver rippled down her spine. Drake did nothing by half-measures. He didn't hold anything back from her—his opinions, his temper, his kindness, his passion. How would it feel to be on the receiving end of that kind of devotion every day?

How did he feel about her? Besides wanting her in the most basic way a man wants a woman?

She feared that due to the intensity of their forced circumstances and heightened emotions what she felt for him wasn't real. She might've romanticized him and this situation. Embellished the idea his touches were highly possessive.

But when she'd remembered his guilt for the difficult decision he'd made tonight, the absolute mastery he'd shown of her body and the sweet tenderness he'd revealed in the aftermath, a hot thrill ran through her.

A pang of regret. No matter how much she'd like to explore the long-term possibilities with Drake, his entrance into her life was a fluke. He'd return to Florida, maybe as soon as tomorrow, if he'd gotten the information he'd needed on Diablo from Tito Cortez.

She'd better make tonight count.

"Kenna?" Bobby said. "We're back at the motel."

She stretched. "Man. Do I need a shower."

The side door slid open. Drake held a hand inside to help her from the van.

Kenna ducked her head and jumped to the concrete, forgetting she'd worn heels. Burning pain shot up her shins. "Ow."

"Steady," Drake murmured, curving his hand against her lower back for support.

Bobby hopped out and closed the door behind him. "Hey boss, we'll be waiting in our room for a debrief."

"I'll be right there."

If the debrief took half as long as the planning, she wouldn't see him until sunup. So much for her seduction plans.

Once Bobby and Geo were a safe distance away, Drake gathered her in his strong arms. "You did great tonight. I know it wasn't easy. Thank you."

"You're welcome."

"You tired?"

"No."

He rubbed his cheek against her forehead. "Hungry?"

Not for vending machine snacks. "Maybe."

He pulled back. When he glanced down into her face, his nostrils flared. "Jesus. Don't look at me like that."

"Like what?"

"Like I'm a midnight snack."

"It's not my fault you didn't feed me." Kenna nipped his chin. Laved the small sting with a saucy flick of her tongue. "And you are pretty tasty."

"Keep it up," he growled, "and I'll throw you up against the van and fuck you right here."

"Mmm. Promise?" She kissed his throat. "You have a thing for sex in public places."

Drake groaned and gave her a small head butt. "What am I going to do with you, hot stuff?"

Keep me.

Oh don't go there. You'll just make it harder on yourself when he walks away. Still, she tightened her hold on him, doubting he noticed.

"I've got to do this debrief right now. I don't know how long it'll take."

"I'll wait up."

Surprise lit his eyes. "Really?"

"Really. But try to put the 'brief' back in debrief, okay?"

He kissed her so sweetly tears stung her lids. No doubt this man was going to break her heart.

They crisscrossed through the cars, motorcycles and trailers. Groups of bikers loitered in the parking lot. Cigarette smoke and laughter hung in the air. No one paid attention to them. They were just another couple calling it a night. It felt nice. Normal.

At the door to their room, Drake kissed her again, longingly, like he couldn't bear to leave her.

"See you in a bit."

••

Kenna woke up when the door to the motel room opened, cutting a silvery swath of moonlight through the darkness. Her gaze flew to the digital clock. She'd crashed more than two hours ago.

Drake said softly, "Kenna?"

"I'm here. Sorry. I fell asleep." Knocking the pillows aside, she scooted back until her shoulders hit the headboard.

"Sorry I woke you."

"Don't be."

"In that case…" He grabbed her ankles and jerked her down the mattress.

She shrieked.

He bounced on the bed beside her. The next thing she knew, he'd hauled her on top of him. His marauding tongue was in her mouth and his hands were everywhere else. Fingertips tracked her spine to her nape. He broke the lip-tingling kiss. "Thank God you got rid of that damn wig."

"Don't you like me as a blonde?"

"I don't like you dressed up as anybody else, period. You're perfect without all the makeup and other junk." Clutching handfuls of her real hair, he brought her mouth back to his.

Happiness burst inside her. Hot, wet, hungry kisses kicked her desire for him until she wriggled and moaned, searching for a firmer contact. He rolled, kneeing her legs apart. The bulge in his jeans ground into her throbbing sex, right where she needed it.

The man knew exactly how to touch her.

"Take your clothes off. Take them off now."

"I still need to take a shower."

"Excellent idea."

Drake levered himself off the bed.

Thud. His boots hit the floor. In the dark she couldn't see him removing his clothes, but she heard it. That purpose-filled rustling was more erotic and intimate than an all out striptease.

His hands were on her shoulders and he lifted her to her feet. "Last chance. Take them off or I tear them off."

"Drake—"

"Do it, Kenna. I want you so bad I can't stand it."

She undressed like her clothes were on fire.

Immediately he rubbed his naked body against hers. "Shower," he said gruffly, "now."

Butterflies danced in her stomach and she retreated a step.

He followed, crowding her. "What? You aren't going all shy on me, are you?"

"Not exactly. It's just…" She sighed. "Umm. Well. I've never showered with a man before." Praise be to the darkness that hid the telltale flush on her cheeks.

"Sweet Jesus. You're trying to kill me, aren't you?"

"What do you mean?"

"This." Drake grabbed her hand and wrapped her fingers around his cock. "I was hard before your little confession. I'm so turned on right now, thinking about being the only man who's ever going to see you naked, wet and slippery."

That's what scared her. The magnification of her flaws. In such a small space they'd be impossible to hide. "Can we leave the lights off?"

His heavy breathing gusted across her cheek when he whispered, "Not a chance in hell. I want to soap every glorious inch of you. Trace the water droplets cascading down your body with my tongue. And when I pin you to the wall and drive into you, I want to watch your face when you come."

Her stomach dipped and swooped like she'd hopped on a roller coaster.

Without another word, he uncurled her fingers from his erection, snagged a condom and tugged her into the bathroom.

"Stand still. Close your eyes."

As soon as she complied, he slipped something silky over her forehead and across her eyes, tying it at the back of her head.

"The blindfold will make sure you can concentrate only on how I make you feel, Kenna. Let me make you feel good."

She heard the shower turn on and water splattering against the plastic shower curtain. Then his hands were guiding her, his body was coaxing her under the deluge.

"Right like this. Hands at your sides."

"But—"

"If you can't promise to keep your hands to yourself I'll go get the cuffs."

"Fine."

"Good girl." He situated her so the hot water hit her chin and flowed down the front of her body.

Kenna sighed. The sigh turned into a moan of delight when he began to massage her back, digging his thumbs into the tight muscles between her shoulders. How did he know exactly where she carried all of her tension?

"Relax."

"I am."

"Liar." He chuckled against her nape and moved his nimble fingers along her spine. His mouth followed, trailing warm kisses over her damp flesh, relaxing her and putting her on edge.

The man was relentless. He rubbed and massaged every muscle, tendon and bone in her back. Plus her neck. Her arms. Her shoulders. She stood under the spray, drowning in his glorious attentions and the steam, finding it difficult to catch her breath.

Right. Drake's wicked mouth and magical hands were causing her to gasp, not the humidity.

He cupped her buttocks. Ground his erection into the soft cleft and growled in her ear, "Touching your slippery body like this is making me think dirty, nasty thoughts, Kenna, about how much I want to slick up my cock and fuck you every possible way known to man and beast. And then make up some new ones no one has ever tried."

She shivered. "Drake—"

"But I've got to get you clean before we can get down and dirty." The abrupt loss of his warm, smooth flesh slipping against hers made her whimper.

Kenna heard him rustling around behind her and tensed up.

A nubby washcloth skated down her spine. "You're supposed to be loose-limbed and mindless after the sensual massage."

"Wrong, you're purposely trying to drive me crazy."

"Glad to see it's working. But I'm far from done. Turn around, hot stuff."

The instant the water hit her back, his mouth devoured hers. He tasted wet and hot and male. She swayed forward, aching to dig her hands, her heels, her teeth, everything into his luscious form. She wanted to wrap her arms and legs around him and ride him under the shower spray until they were both spent and the water ran cold.

He pulled back. "Ah-ah, you're distracting me. Don't rush this. Just feel."

Was this his way of giving her something to remember him by before he disappeared from her life forever?

She didn't dwell on it. All coherent thoughts vanished as Drake dragged the sudsy washcloth over her collarbone. He slowed down and her senses sharpened. The pine-scented soap seemed more pungent. The lather caressing her skin was more luxurious.

His breathing became labored and echoed in the small space with each new drawn-out touch he bestowed upon her.

Kenna caught the spicy scent of her own arousal, felt the cream thickening in her core, then sliding down the inside of her trembling thighs. Her body was ready and eager for the next step in this mating dance. What was he waiting for?

Drake took his own sweet time washing her breasts. Her nipples seemed to be especially dirty. As he inched his way down her torso, she quivered. Although the water flowing over her skin was hot, it seemed ice cold in comparison to the blood that'd reached the boiling point inside her.

"You're tensing up again."

"Please. I can't take any more water games. I'm going to come without you in about two seconds. I'd rather come with you, Drake. Please."

The washcloth hit the tub and Drake's hungry mouth swooped down in a harsh kiss. Her arms snaked around his neck and she lost her mind to pure sexual greed when her hard nipples and soft breasts connected with the firm wall of his chest.

Drake groaned in the back of his throat before picking her up, spinning her around and pressing her against the cold back wall.

He spread her knees wide, tipped her hips forward and ripped off the blindfold the same time he drove into her.

Kenna came immediately, a wet, throbbing supercharged explosion: a rainbow of light in her head, the taste of Drake on her tongue and the thrilling sound of his release in her ear.

After she'd caught her breath, Drake nuzzled the side of her neck. "Just think. I still have to wash your hair."

••

An hour later, her skin wrinkled and water dripping down her face, Kenna clutched Drake's muscular ass as he coaxed a third screaming orgasm from her. Oh what a marvelous way to lose her shower virginity.

••

Drake suspected Kenna was up to something.

After the vigorous session in the shower, he thought he'd be sated, for a while at least. But they'd barely made it to the bed and he was hard again. He'd made love to her unhurriedly, lost in her tiny whimpers of delight and the way she'd given herself to him without reservation. Frankly, it amazed him she hadn't complained about his voracious appetite for her. Once he'd realized she hadn't had much experience in making love—were all the men in South Dakota total idiots?—her complete surrender to him was even sweeter.

Entwined comfortably like longtime lovers, they'd spent the last few hours talking, touching, laughing. Strange, that he knew more about her after spending only two days together than he did with most people whom he'd known for years.

Why had their connection been so instantaneous? From the moment he'd seen her, he'd become…obsessed. He couldn't touch her enough. Goad her enough. Drake wanted to crawl inside her brain and learn her secrets. This wasn't normal behavior. He'd prided himself on a certain aloofness where his job was concerned.

She wasn't just a job. Hadn't been from day one.

Deep down he knew he couldn't blame their immediate bond on the intensity of the situation. He'd been thrust into scenarios exactly like this one more times than he could count. Sometimes, even with a beautiful woman. But he'd never felt or acted this crazed and out of control.

Dammit. What was this elusive feeling of possessiveness and satisfaction mixed with an overwhelming sense of need every time he looked at Kenna?

It hit him like a freight train. Love.

Shit. He'd never been in love, no wonder he hadn't recognized the signs.

But he was in love with her. He repeated the phrase to himself, I love her. Relief loosened the knots in his stomach and a strange calm settled over him. Drake always suspected that when he fell for a woman, he'd fall hard. And fast. With Kenna, he knew he'd be wiping the dust off his ass for the next fifty or sixty years from the sheer force of the fall.

He grinned. No question she belonged with him, even if she hadn't realized it yet. He'd make her see things his way. One thing he knew how to do was execute a successful plan. She didn't stand a chance.

"Drake?" Kenna murmured. "You asleep?"

"No."

Her soft cool fingers lazily zigzagged down his belly. Lingered on the line of hair between his hipbones.

His cock began to stir.

A throaty laugh tickled his ear. "You are insatiable, secret agent man."

"Only with you."

"Does that mean you trust me?"

Kenna seemed overly anxious for his answer and he wondered again what she was up to. He said mildly, "Yeah, I suppose I do."

She moved faster than he'd anticipated. Straddling his waist, she smoothed her palms up his torso, down his arms until she reached his wrists. The pillows tumbled to the floor as she pulled his arms above his head and pinned them to the mattress.

"We both know I can't make you stay like this. And you'd never let me use your precious cuffs, so handcuffing you to the bed isn't an option either." She nibbled the shell of his ear fully aware it drove him insane. "So I'm asking you nicely, Drake. Keep your hands right here."

A small kernel of unease unfurled. "Why?"

"You didn't think you'd get away unscathed for letting those guys cop a feel at the meeting tonight, did you? You need to learn I also have consequences for bad decisions."

Every muscle in his body went rigid; one muscle in particular.

"Let me touch you," she whispered. "I promise it won't hurt."

Like he could refuse.

Kenna gently kissed his forehead, his cheeks, his eyelids and finally his mouth. Teeth nipped his jawbone, her tongue traced the cords straining in his neck. She peppered kisses over his chest, murmuring admiration for his rock-hard pecs. When she suckled his nipple, pleasure speared through him like a burning lance and his hands automatically came up to clutch her silky hair.

"Uh-uh. I'll stop if you don't put those interfering mitts back where they belong, Agent March."

Needless to say, he complied.

Her wet tongue outlined every ripple in his abs with painstaking precision. A playful nip on each hipbone and she only had one other place to go.

Down.

Drake held his breath.

A delicate lick circled the crown of his cock. He managed to keep his decorum until she slid that swollen part of him all the way into her warm mouth.

"Holy mother of God." His hips arched off the bed.

Kenna released him, an inch at a time, paused and sucked him back inside that moist heated cavern until the tip hit the back of her throat. With her mouth and hands, she created a rhythm that made him thrash on the bed like an animal caught in a trap. His balls drew tight, he braced himself for the detonation.

Then she stopped entirely. "Hold still."

He'd never let a woman have such control. Not that he particularly liked being powerless, but the sensations coursing through him were too potent to complain. So he waited. Sweat trickling down his temple. Heart beating wildly. His hands clenched in fists above his head. His dick as hard as granite.

Her hand spread a cool gel-like substance over his cock from root to tip. She pumped up and down while just the tip of her tongue circled his nipple.

He closed his eyes. Jesus that felt good. Icy coldness changed to heat. His dick began to tingle. When her hot mouth closed over him again, heightening the temperature change, he couldn't stand it another minute. He whimpered, "Please," and hoped he didn't sound like a whiny, needy fool.

"Please what?"

"Finish it."

"With my mouth or my hands?"

"Your mouth."

"Sit up and look at me."

Drake managed to lift his head.

"No colored contacts, no wig, just me this time, Drake. I want to watch you come so you know who brought you there."

He propped himself on his elbow and cupped her head in his hand, gentling his thumb across her cheekbone. "Believe me, I know who you are." *The woman I love,* he added silently, knowing if he declared his feelings now, she'd think it was only because she'd given him a killer blowjob.

But he would tell her. Tomorrow.

"Good. You'd better not hold back." Locking their gazes, she took him deep.

"Jesus."

His hips pumped. His head spun. He doubted his cock could get any harder. Her wet, sucking sounds filled the air, stoking the fire inside him to an inferno. The sweet scent of her desire, of sex, of her skin and hair surrounded him like a fragrant cloud. Once again she drove him to that ragged edge but instead of pulling him back, she sent him flying over.

He was weightless. Mindless. Existing only in that moment of pure bliss.

Drake felt the clasp of her lips around his cock as he exploded in her mouth, felt her throat working as she swallowed. His entire body shook from the force of his climax.

Spent, he sagged to the mattress. But he found the strength to reach for her, needing her as an anchor now more than ever.

Kenna snuggled up beside him. "That was fun. But next time I go to a sex toy store, I might pick up a paddle."

"A paddle?" he said hoarsely. "For what?"

"Spanking, I guess."

"You're not gonna spank me. *Ever.*"

"Then I guess next time I ask, you'd better let me use your handcuffs."

Oh yeah. He definitely loved this woman.

Chapter Sixteen

Somewhere near dawn Drake murmured, "We need to talk sometime today, okay?"

She'd been lolling in another rosy afterglow, but his words snapped her wide awake. "Um, sure," she mumbled, hoping he couldn't feel the sudden tension tightening her body.

What did he want to talk about? Although he hadn't given her any details on his meeting with Tito Cortez, she'd gotten the impression he had the information he'd needed. Which meant he had no reason to stick around.

She choked back a sudden rush of tears. Although she'd known the outcome of this affair from the beginning, nothing had prepared her for this feeling of absolute devastation.

God. What an idiot. She'd fallen in love with him.

Don't cry. Kenna focused on the sunlight creeping through the crack in the drapes, wondering if she'd ever have a peaceful night's sleep again. But exhaustion eventually won out and she dozed off.

The phone rang. Drake cursed and rolled over. Snatching the receiver, he barked into it, "What?" He paused. "Ah hell. No. That's all right. Tell them we'll be right there."

He sighed and replaced the receiver.

She gathered the sheet around her nakedness. "What's up?"

"Drug deal gone bad. Guess they had the same thing happen last year so the local DEA has requested our help."

"They know you're here?"

"Yeah. Standard procedure. Jurisdictional issues and all that political crap." He dry washed his face. "I gotta go. You go back to sleep. Bobby'll still be here tying up loose ends if you need anything." His mouth connected with hers briefly. He stretched and looked at her with regret. "I like waking up with you in my arms."

Her grip on the sheet increased. "I sense a 'but'."

"But I'd hoped we'd have more time together this morning. Not just to make love again"—he grinned—"not that I wouldn't be up for it. We'll talk when I get back."

Five minutes later he was gone.

Kenna glanced at the clock. She couldn't fall back asleep. By noon she'd showered, packed and suffered through enough daytime TV. Grabbing her purse, she headed toward Bobby's room.

He opened the door right after she knocked. "Kenna! Come on in. The boss said you'd be by."

Papers were strewn across the unmade bed. "Am I bugging you?"

"Nah." He ushered her to the chair. "Just finishing up my reports. Actually, they're Geo's reports, but he pawns them off on me."

"Why?"

"Because he can. He's the senior field officer and I'm just a lowly rookie." Bobby gave her a crooked smile. "I don't mind. I'm damn lucky I got assigned to this team."

He'd provided her with the perfect opportunity to fish for information on Drake. "Have you worked with Agent March for long?"

"Long enough to see why he's considered the best agent around. The man is relentless."

He didn't have to tell her about Drake's stamina. "Do you get a break once this case is wrapped up?"

"Are you kidding me? I'm sure the boss has already lined up twelve more ops just like this one."

An uneasy feeling began to stir. Was she just another case number in the busy life of a DEA agent? "Sounds like the cases are all the same."

"Pretty much. After a while they all blend together. Of course, every case has its own challenges. Doesn't matter to Agent March since he thrives on challenge." His blue eyes lit with admiration. "He's an absolute master at getting people to do what he wants, even if they don't want to do it. Before they know what hit them, they fall in line, exactly like he'd planned."

Just like me.

The hard truth punched a hole in her hope. She'd been nothing more than a challenge to uber spy Agent March. Certainly she'd proven herself to be a total pushover, not only where the case with Jerry Travis and Diablo was concerned, but personally. The minute he'd touched her, she'd melted in his arms like an ice cream cone in the August sun.

Another thought popped up. If he was a master manipulator, he probably could bluff with the best of them too. He probably had no authority to turn her over to the IRS. Or the Meade County sheriff.

God, how had she been so stupid to fall for that line of bullshit?

She had to get out of here now, before Drake returned and gave her his (probably) well-practiced good-bye-it's-been-fun-speech.

Smiling at Bobby, even though she was seething inside, she eased from the chair and stretched. "Well. I'll let you get back to the grindstone."

He frowned. "You okay?"

"Just tired. I might sneak in another catnap before Agent March gets back."

"Wish I could," he grumbled.

Her sweaty fingers fumbled with the doorknob. "See ya."

She managed to casually stroll back to her room when she wanted to run. Inside the dark space, the scent of sex and Drake lingered. She had to get out of here. She debated on using the motel phone or the pay phone. No time to waste. Dropping her duffel bag on the floor, she picked up the receiver and dialed.

Kenna cursed and hung up. She still hadn't heard from Shawnee and obviously Shawnee hadn't replaced her cell phone. She dialed another number.

Relief swept through her when Marissa answered on the second ring. "Thank God I caught you. Can you come and pick me up? Right now. I'm at the Sunset Motel on Highway 385. Okay. No, I haven't heard from Tito Cortez yet." She listened to Marissa's line of logic. "Because I honestly don't think I can go through with it tonight. Fine. We'll talk about it when you get here. But please, hurry."

Kenna skulked around the edges of the parking lot, worried Drake would return before she made her escape. Marissa warned her to be on the lookout for a different vehicle since her car was in the repair shop.

A white Ford Taurus pulled up to the curb.

"Let me help you load your stuff," Marissa said brusquely. She skirted the trunk, opened the passenger door and then threw the duffel bag and Kenna's purse in the backseat.

Once seated, Kenna automatically reached for her seatbelt. That's when she realized Marissa hadn't budged. She looked up and liquid fear raced through her blood.

Marissa pointed a gun at her.

"Is this a joke?"

"No. Move over. You're driving."

Despite the shock, she swallowed several times before she managed to ask, "Marissa what's going on? What are you doing?"

"Finishing what I started. Now drive."

"Where?"

"I'm taking you to meet Tito Cortez."

••

Drake went into a rage when he returned to the motel and found Kenna gone.

No note. No message at the front desk. Nothing. She'd just skipped out without a word.

He grilled Bobby for details on Kenna's mood. When Bobby relayed their conversation, Drake had a better idea on why she'd bolted. Question was: Where had she run?

After calling her home phone half a dozen times, he drove the van over to check her apartment. Although her car was still there, she wouldn't answer the door. That wasn't like Kenna. If she wanted to tell him to go to hell, she'd have done it right to his face. Hiding out wasn't her style.

Maybe she was staying at Marissa's place.

He stopped in the manager's office.

A shaggy-haired college student with blood-shot eyes emerged from the back room. "Can I help ya, man?"

"Possibly. I'm supposed to meet Marissa Cruz, but she forgot to give me her apartment number." Drake leaned on the counter, the picture of sincerity. "I know you're not supposed to give out that information, but I was wondering if you'd seen Marissa hanging around today?"

"Nope. I ain't seen her since she gave her notice two weeks ago."

Had Kenna known Marissa planned on moving? "Guess I could check with her friend Kenna."

The boy blinked. "Who?"

Error. No one knew her as Kenna except him. "Kaye Anne Ennis. She lives in 17C?"

"Oh her." He yawned.

"She been around this afternoon?"

"Nah." Scratching the red stubble on his chin, he said, "Well, maybe. I dunno. She ain't exactly the type of woman that sticks out, know what I mean?"

Drake refrained from grabbing the clueless bastard by his baggy hemp shirt and shaking him until his roach clip fell out of his cargo pants. "So you haven't seen her today?"

"Nope."

"What about her roommate, Shawnee?"

"No. I'da remembered seeing that hot-looking Indian babe."

When the phone rang Drake left.

He paused inside the courtyard, at a loss to where Kenna could have gone. After a few minutes of pacing, he sat on the concrete bench and considered his options.

Two pig-tailed girls in polka-dotted swimsuits raced past. Then a young couple holding hands, dragging a double-sized water float. A whistling Native American man walked by, long hair flowing loosely down his back, swinging his towel, also headed for the pool.

Drake's head snapped. Wait a second. It was that son of a bitch Trent.

He stood and followed him for a few feet, resisting the urge to tackle him. Instead he shouted, "Mr. Eagle? Can I talk to you?"

Without looking his way, Trent tossed his towel and started to run.

Shit. He might have to tackle him anyway.

But Trent's flip-flops tripped him and he fell ass over teakettle in the grass.

Before Drake could help him up, Trent crab-crawled backward. "You can keep chasing me, but I don't know how many times I have to tell you. I don't have the money!"

"What the hell are you talking about?"

Trent cocked his head. "Aren't you one of those goons with the credit collection agency?"

"No. I'm with the DEA and I'm looking for Kenna—I mean Kaye Ennis. Have you seen her?"

"Not if I can help it." He scooted back further, fear on his face. "She sicced the DEA on me? Even after I swore to that bitch Shawnee I'd never do it again?"

"Do what?"

"Shawnee almost broke my goddamn arm when she found out what I'd done."

Was this guy on drugs? "What exactly did you do?"

"Don't act like you don't know. That's why you're here, isn't it? The grant application last year."

Drake nodded. "Start talking."

"When I dated Shawnee I ended up with a key to Shawnee and Kaye's mailbox. After Shawnee told me Kaye and I had applied for the same grant, I kept an eye on her mail and destroyed the follow-up letter from the DEA requesting more financial information. The deadline passed. And I got the grant."

"Why was Drug Enforcement contacting you?"

Trent blinked. "Drug Enforcement? What are you talking about?" His eyes narrowed. "I'm talking about DEA. Douglas Endowment Alliance. They're the grant foundation."

"Shit."

"Who are you?"

Drake shoved a hand through his hair. What a complete fuck-up. "Someone who has got to find her. Like now."

"Why? Is Kaye in trouble with Drug Enforcement?"

Drake didn't care for the sudden glint in Trent's eye. "No, Kaye isn't in trouble with Drug Enforcement, but you still haven't answered my first question. Have you seen her?"

"No."

"Second question: Where were you at ten-thirty, night before last?"

"Am I under arrest?"

"No."

Smugly he retorted, "Then I don't have to tell you."

Drake hunkered down. Got his mean on. "Yes, you do. And if you don't start talking I'll do way more than break your goddamn arm."

"Okay, okay, fine." His Dudley Do-Right chin came up. "No shame in being an honest working man. I worked the graveyard shift at Perkins in Spearfish."

"Your supervisor can verify it?"

"Yes. I clocked in at nine-forty-five and out at six-thirty a.m. No break. We're slammed during the Rally."

There went his number one shooting suspect. "Question three: Did you sabotage Kenna – I mean Kaye's application this year?"

"Hell no. Shawnee would gut me like a trout. You might think you're scary, but I guarantee I'd rather tangle with you than her." He shuddered.

"Don't bet on it." Drake turned and walked off.

Frustrated, Drake headed back to the motel. He prowled the room, building and discarding Kenna's motives for taking off.

How could Kenna think, even for a second, that she was just another case in a long line of cases? Didn't she know she was special?

Finally the part of his brain that wasn't controlled by his cock spoke up. No, she didn't know how he felt, because he hadn't bothered to tell her.

Christ. He was such a moron.

Two hours passed. He paced, his gut instinct told him something was seriously wrong. With his apprehension growing, he tasked Geo to help him while Bobby retrieved the motorcycle and camping gear from the Broken Arrow.

When Geo tracked down the number Kenna had called from the motel phone, Drake wasn't surprised to learn it was Marissa's cell phone. Marissa didn't answer. He didn't like, nor did he trust that woman. Anyone who would encourage a friend to act as a "tour guide" aka a high priced escort—

His stomach plummeted like a rock. Surely, after everything he'd told her, everything she'd seen last night, Kenna hadn't agreed to squire around Tito Cortez. He recalled cash passed between Tito and Marissa. What had that been about? Had Tito given her a deposit on Kenna's services?

But that meant Kenna had planned on taking off all along.

He didn't believe it. They'd connected on a whole different level last night. Even the most jaded woman would have a hard time walking away and Kenna didn't have a callous bone in her body. Stubborn, yes. Determined, yes, but never spiteful.

How had he forgotten her determination to earn the cash to pay her tuition? She'd told him she'd do whatever it took.

Including sacrificing her dignity and willingly placing herself in the hands of a suspected drug dealer?

Not if he could help it. But how the hell was he supposed to find her when she'd proven she could hide in plain sight? He hadn't a clue how many different disguises she had crammed in her duffel bag.

Bag. Purse. An idea clicked like a missing puzzle piece.

Drake ran down the sidewalk and pounded on Geo and Bobby's door. When Bobby answered, he grabbed Bobby by the polo shirt and demanded, "Did you remove the tracker from Kenna's purse last night in the van after the op like I told you?"

Bobby's face burned beet red at Drake's apparent fury. "No, sir. I meant to, but since we didn't need to use it, I-I forgot."

"Thank God." In his jubilation, he gave Bobby a loud smacking kiss on the forehead. "I owe you, buddy. Turn it on. Let's find Kenna so I can wring her neck."

••

Besides the tersely given directions, Marissa hadn't spoken. Kenna had driven them to a vacant veterinary clinic on the outskirts of town. A "For Sale" sign nestled in the corner of the dirty windows, the faded name and number of a realty company listed on the bottom. The realty company Marissa worked for.

Not a car in the gravel parking lot. The metal chutes for loading large livestock were rusted open from disuse.

Tumbleweeds had gathered in the arched entryway. Red dust covered everything.

After snatching the car keys, Marissa hauled Kenna out of the car, keeping the gun in the small of her back. "Here's the master key. Unlock the door."

Kenna's hand shook. "What are we doing here?"

"You'll find out soon enough. Open the damn door. And don't try to run once we get inside because I will shoot you."

The metal hinges creaked when Kenna jerked on the handle. The stale odor of animal urine rushed out and she gagged.

"Inside."

Marissa pushed her and slammed the door shut. Prodding her with the gun, they walked through a labyrinth of muddy hallways. There were doors everywhere. Even if Kenna unearthed her courage and tried to escape, she'd waste precious time trying to find a way out of the building.

Cold fear slammed into her.

At the end of a corridor, they entered a cavernous room two stories high. It stank of manure and feed and motor oil. Despite the darkness, Kenna looked around for a place to hide. Rows of individual stalls lined the wall opposite the garage door. A variety of hooks and rusted-out pulleys dangled from the ceiling above each stall, an area she remembered from her ranch days that was used for surgery for large animals. Built-in plywood shelves were stacked from the concrete floor to a raised platform nestled in the far corner.

Unfortunately, the only windows were on the top level above the loft. No one could see in. She couldn't see out.

Two straight-backed, paint-chipped chairs had been placed in the center of the room. Marissa kicked aside a burlap bag and pointed with the gun to the chair on the left. "Sit."

Kenna sat.

From the bag, Marissa pulled out a roll of duct tape. She placed it on Kenna's knee. "Wrap that tape around your calf and the chair leg. Right one first."

"You're making me tie myself up?"

Marissa grinned evilly. "Yeah. And if you make a break for it, I'll shoot you in the thigh first, then work my way up."

Once Kenna finished, she straightened until her spine connected with the back of the chair.

"Clasp your hands behind your back."

She did as instructed, holding her breath as Marissa stalked closer. Some strangely brave section of her brain knew Marissa had to put the gun down in order to tie her hands and it insanely insisted she grab the opportunity to escape. But fear overrode the erratic impulse. She remained absolutely still while Marissa wound duct tape around her wrists.

Marissa stepped in front of her again, gun in one hand, cell phone in the other. "Here's what we're gonna do. You're going to convince Tito Cortez that you couldn't wait until tonight to see him. Naturally he'll get suspicious, then you'll tearfully admit you've been ditched by your lover out in the middle of nowhere and beg him to hop on his bike to pick you up. Men get off on that coming to the rescue shit." Her cold brown eyes narrowed. "The bike part is important because I want him alone. I don't want any of his Compadres buddies or bodyguards tagging along."

"And if I can't convince him?"

"You will if you want to live."

Bile rose in her throat. "What happens then?"

"Then I show up at the meeting in your place and bring him back here." Marissa punched in a number. "Hope your acting skills are good because your life depends on it." She held the receiver to Kenna's ear and the gun at the back of her head.

The barrel was cold in comparison to the sweat pouring down her neck.

"Remember, I can hear every word. I've waited too damn long for this. You tip him off, you die."

With that threat hanging over her head, Kenna had no problem persuading Tito to her meet early.

As Marissa clipped the phone back on her belt, Kenna found the courage she'd been lacking.

"I thought we were friends."

"Wrong. We were never friends."

"So you decided to kidnap me and tie me up to prove it?"

"No. You've been nothing more than bait. Tito is so predictable. He's such a sucker for a blonde with big tits."

"Bait?"

"For someone who's supposedly so smart, you sure are dumb, *Kenna*." She said the name sarcastically. "Last year Jerry and I planned to intercept a huge shipment from Jerry's boss. He needed an alibi. You were it. Ten grand was a small price to pay when our haul was over two million. His boss blamed it on another motorcycle club. Some ragtag bunch of Indians on the reservation who think they've got the stones to play in the big leagues. We got away free." Marissa laughed again.

"Why me?"

"Because you're desperate. Not only for the cash, but you need to prove you're not a good girl. That you're wild. That you'll hire yourself out as a 'tour guide'...please. Did you really believe that hot, gorgeous girls become companions to lonely men all in innocent fun? Do you have any idea what really goes on at escort services?" She paused. "Those women are whores, bought and paid for just like the ones working the corners. The only difference is they don't have to fuck their customers in a filthy alley."

Kenna had suspected. But she'd been so grateful to have the cash for tuition she'd rather stupidly decided not to look a gift horse in the mouth.

"Cheer up. You're not the only gullible one. That smug bastard Tito doesn't know that I figured out he and Jerry double-crossed me. But he will. Soon."

Kenna cringed when Marissa stepped forward, a malicious gleam in her eye.

Pain exploded in her head and everything went dark.

CHAPTER SEVENTEEN

A door slammed, nudging Kenna back to reality.

Marissa pushed Tito Cortez into view through the dimly lit doorway. She held the gun to his temple and walked sideways beside him. With his ankles wrapped in duct tape, he shuffled across the floor like a crippled old man. He stumbled; Marissa righted his balance by yanking on the handcuffs behind his back. She shoved him in the chair, secured him with more tape, then punched him in the face.

Kenna heard the sickening crack of bone breaking.

The strip of silver tape muffled Tito's immediate cry of pain. Blood began to pour out his nose and Kenna found she couldn't look away from the horror, knowing Marissa would do that, or something worse, to her.

"Now that we're all here, let's get the party started." She reached over and ripped the tape from Tito's mouth.

"You fucking crazy bitch, I'll kill you for this!"

"You're not exactly in the position to be calling me names, Cortez." She smirked. "What happened to the big badass Compadres gang member everybody is afraid of, hmmm?"

He spit blood on the floor. "You'd never have gotten the drop on me, cunt, if you hadn't used your pussy stun gun on me first."

Marissa rolled her eyes at Kenna. "Men have such a problem being outsmarted by a woman, don't you think?"

Kenna didn't dare nod.

"You're not nearly as smart as you think you are," he sneered.

"I'm not the one bleeding and trussed up like a pig for slaughter." Marissa spun and disappeared into the shadows only to return with another chair. She flipped it around, straddled it and rested her forearm on the back. The gun was pointed at Tito's groin. "Now. When did you and Jerry Travis decide to double-cross me and take over Diablo?"

Kenna jerked in her seat. God. Marissa was involved with Diablo?

Tito didn't say a word.

"I knew Jerry had a partner. I was just surprised it was you." She angled her head and studied him.

Something resembling a snort sounded from Tito's broken nose.

Marissa rose slowly to stand in front of him. Whacked him in the side of the head with the gun grip with enough force his head snapped back. Once Tito had quit swearing at her, she calmly said, "I'm asking again. What did Jerry tell the DEA about Diablo?"

"Why didn't you ask Jerry?"

"I did. He wouldn't tell me so I killed him. I tortured him first, though. Some partner. He rolled on you right away."

Although the woman in front of her looked like Marissa and talked like her, there wasn't a trace of the woman Kenna had known and it scared her to the bone. She knew she was going to die.

Tito glared at Kenna as if noticing her for the first time. "Why is she here?"

"Bait. Knew I couldn't get you alone unless I dangled a whore in front of you."

"I am not a whore," Kenna said.

Marissa stared at her and laughed. "You took money from a man for the pleasure of your company. Doesn't matter if you spread your legs for him or not." She sauntered over to Kenna, her free hand smoothed over her scalp. "Sorry, if the truth upsets you, *amiga*."

"Get your hands off me."

Marissa cuffed her with the gun barrel.

Her vision wavered. She wanted to throw up from the pain.

Tito laughed. "You are one cold bitch, Cruz."

Marissa's brown eyes were as flat and emotionless as her tone. "You got that right."

"Maybe we can strike a deal after all."

"Too late," she snapped. "Diablo is mine. I proved I have the *cajones* to run with the big boys. Took me two years of living in this little shit-hole town to get it organized." She began to pace. "Jerry told me everything I needed, including his boss's transportation schedule from Miami. And after some persuasion, he gave me all the details on the distribution network across the Midwest. Technically I don't need you. But I do want to know how much the DEA knows about my plans."

Tito actually looked scared for the first time.

Kenna dry heaved. The violent, unrelenting stranger she'd considered a friend would kill them both without remorse.

Marissa thumbed the safety. "Last chance, Cortez."

His mouth twisted in a grotesque sneer. "You ain't gonna shoot me. The last thing you want is the wrath of the Compadres on your foolish head. You're bluffing, *puta*."

The gunshot was deafening. Almost as deafening as Tito's answering scream.

When the smoke cleared, Kenna saw blood pouring down his right arm and over the spider tattoo.

Marissa said, "I never bluff."

••

Geo had finally pinpointed Kenna's location. Drake raced off on the motorcycle, armed, angry, and wondering what the hell she was doing more than two miles out of town. Traffic leading out of Sturgis on this deserted service road wasn't bad. Still, by the time he'd hit the open road, he'd reached the boiling point.

Following the coordinates on the portable GPS, he sped past the abandoned veterinary building. A mile up the road he stopped, called Geo and double-checked the coordinates. The signal from the tracker on Kenna's purse hadn't moved. He'd been in the right place after all.

Hot, dry winds whipped powdery patches of dirt along the highway into red dust devils. The strength of the gusts nearly blew the motorcycle off the road. When Drake reached the vast parking lot surrounding the veterinary building, he powered down the bike and rolled it into a shallow drainage ditch. Probably overly cautious, but he had no way of knowing what was going on inside and wasn't about to broadcast his presence.

He loaded the clip in his Glock, shoved the extra clip inside his vest and turned his cell phone to vibrate. He moved toward the Ford Taurus parked behind the building.

At least the gale force of the wind masked the sound of the gravel crunching beneath his boots. He hunkered down in the shadow of the car, raising his head up only far enough to peek inside the driver's side window. Nothing out of the ordinary besides the rental sticker. He shuffled to the rear door and looked in the backseat.

The hair on the back of his neck stood up.

Kenna's duffel bag and purse were on the floorboards. Had she sent her belongings with someone else, hoping to throw him off? No. Kenna had no idea Bobby had placed a tracker on her purse. And chances were slim she'd been mugged and the assailant had taken off with her stuff.

So where the hell was she? Why had she chosen to hide out in this spot? He scanned the secluded area and it hit him: No one in his or her right mind would willingly choose to come here.

Someone had forced her here.

Who?

Fear took root, spurring him into action. Using the shadows cast by the waning sunlight, he circled the building and counted five entrances. Main one in the front. Two garage doors in the back. One emergency exit on each side of the structure. All locked, all obvious. The last one had potential. It wasn't a metal door, but a wooden one that connected the outdoor animal chutes with the inside and probably ended up as a direct link to the stalls.

But he had to see the interior layout to make sure. A bank of dirty windows was nestled beneath the roofline. If he could just get up there and look inside… His eyes narrowed on the six-inch pipe running up the side of the building. Encased in metal latticework, it had a wide enough base he could climb. It'd be a stretch to get close to the window. With no other option and running out of time, Drake jammed his gun in the holster and quietly started his ascent.

Sweat poured in his eyes. The muscles in his back protested but he finally reached the top.

Don't look down.

He took a minute to catch his breath, securing his footing on a bracket. Holding on to the pipe with one hand, he leaned out as far as he could and gripped the thin metal strip of the window frame. Even with his face pressed against the filthy glass the interior was so dark he couldn't see anything.

Drake cupped his hand to block the sunlight and waited impatiently for his eyes to adjust. He made out a platform directly below the windows, beyond that stood the hulking forms of the cargo doors.

His gaze traveled down the steel door tracks until it reached the concrete floor and the main body of the room. He squinted until the three figures in the center came into focus. Two sat on chairs, one paced between them. The person standing was definitely a woman, but she wasn't Kenna. Long, lean body, long dark hair.

Was it her roommate, Shawnee?

He watched closely.

When she flicked the long wavy hair over her shoulder, he recognized the twitchy gesture.

Marissa Cruz.

Everything inside him froze. He knew one of the occupants of those chairs had to be Kenna. But which one? He couldn't see because Marissa blocked his view. Nothing blocked his view of the gun in her hand absorbing the kickback as she fired.

Oh Jesus. Oh God. Not Kenna.

Drake flinched and lost his balance. The bracket beneath his foot gave way and plummeted to the concrete, landing with a loud *ping*. Flailing his arm, he swung away from the window in a last-ditch attempt to restore his stability.

Shit. Now he dangled by one hand more than two stories above the ground.

Don't look down.

He gritted his teeth against the excruciating pain of his arm trying to separate from his shoulder socket and lunged for the pipe with his free hand. His fingers connected with the metal, as did his forehead.

Stars exploded inside his head. Cymbals crashed in his ears. Still he hung on. Without waiting for his vision to return, he shinnied down the pipe.

As he hit the ground running, he reached for his cell phone and hit redial. "Geo! Shots were fired inside the building at the coordinates. Request back up immediately. Have them send everything they've got, but goddamn it, make sure they don't come in sirens blaring. There are hostages in there." He swore and snarled, "No, I'm not waiting. I'm going in."

Drake traded the cell phone for his gun. He picked up a broken metal bar and raced to the front entrance. To create a diversion, he beat on the door several times and then backtracked to the rear of the building. Marissa wouldn't ignore the interruption. Hopefully it'd give him enough time to get inside.

Using the sharp flat side of the metal bar, he pried the wooden door until the frame splintered and the rusty hinges shrieked. Too late to worry about giving away his location.

The pungent smell of rotting hay and animal shit permeated the dank space. He crept to the side of the stall and moved toward the release gate. It'd been left open. He craned his neck until he could see the people in the middle of the room.

The breath left his lungs in a *whoosh*.

Kenna was bound to one chair, Tito Cortez to the other. Although blood pooled beneath Tito's chair, revealing he was the one who'd been shot, Kenna's face had seen the business end of a pistol. More than once.

Dark fury seized him.

Where was that bitch Marissa?

She stalked toward Kenna and grabbed her by the hair. She held a knife at Kenna's throat. "I know someone is in here. Come out right now or I swear I'll kill them both. Her first."

Drake gauged his chances of taking Marissa out. Not good with his arm still shaking from his unexpected gymnastics session.

Shit. "How do I know that as soon as I show myself you won't kill them anyway?" he shouted.

"You don't. Show yourself."

He stood and walked out of the stall slowly, keeping his gun above his head. He couldn't look at Kenna or he'd go berserk.

Marissa smirked. "Mr. Mayhaven. Put the piece down." He did. "Now strip." When Drake balked, she dug the knife deeper into Kenna's throat. "Do it or she dies. It's the only way I can be certain you aren't hiding any surprises."

In angry jerky movements, Drake removed his clothes. When he wore nothing but black boxers, she said, "Enough. Stay right there. Now, tell me. How did you get here?"

Drake's eyes flicked to Cortez. "I've been shadowing him."

"Why?"

This was the part where he'd get tripped up if he was wrong. "Jerry told me everything. And when he wound up dead, I figured it was a Compadres hit, so Cortez could take over."

"Well, you figured wrong. I took Jerry out."

Holy shit. Who was this woman?

"Tell me exactly how you 'fell' into this opportunity with Jerry," Marissa demanded.

"Jerry wanted me to use my connections with Vasquez to increase distribution lines, but I didn't trust him because he wouldn't tell me who his partners were in Diablo."

"Partners." Marissa spit on the ground. "Diablo has always been a solo operation. *My* solo operation. Jerry wouldn't have told you anything, unless…"

Tito's head snapped up. "Fuck you, man. You're DEA."

CHAPTER EIGHTEEN

Drake neither confirmed nor denied. But he saw his years' worth of undercover work blown wide open.

And Tito Cortez couldn't walk out of here alive. He glanced at Kenna. Her eyes were large with fear. He'd never wanted her to know the horrors his job entailed. But if he had the chance, he'd kill Marissa and Tito right in front of her to save her life.

"Don't hurt him," Kenna pleaded. "The only reason he's here is because I kept in contact with Jerry over the last year."

Marissa's eyes went cold. "You did? Why?"

"He asked me to do three favors for him."

"What kind of favors?"

"He sent me some packages from Florida. I repacked them and dropped them off where he told me to."

Shit. Kenna had been the courier doing Jerry's dirty work. No wonder she'd looked so spooked when he'd asked her why Jerry had paid her an additional three grand over the last year.

"What was in the packages?" Marissa demanded.

Kenna bit her lip. "I-I don't know. I didn't want to know. I just did what he told me."

"You stupid bitch." Marissa turned and kicked over Kenna's chair. Kenna went down so quickly she didn't have time to scream.

A sickening thud echoed as her head smacked into the ground. Then nothing.

Drake went absolutely rigid.

"Guess I don't need you anymore. *Adios,* asshole." Marissa calmly sited Tito's chest and pumped five bullets into him.

She'd given Drake a small window of opportunity. Despite the ringing in his ears from close range gunfire, he hunkered down and tackled her. The gun flew from her hand and skittered into the shadows. Marissa shrieked. They crashed to the floor.

Marissa kicked and clawed at him, tried to bite his arm. She rammed her knee into his sternum. In the split second he gave in to the pain, she scrambled for her gun.

Drake knew his Glock was somewhere behind him. He scooted backward, over his clothes. His foot connected with the cool metal and he was back on his feet, gun in hand.

But he was too late.

Marissa had retrieved her gun, too. She hadn't aimed it at him; she'd pointed it at Kenna's head.

It required every ounce of concentration to remember his training. Hard to do with his entrails crawling up his throat and his brain paralyzed with fear. If Kenna died, it'd be his fault. He'd never forgive himself. Marissa might as well put a bullet in his head too.

"Drop it. Or I'll kill her."

Drake crouched and set his gun on the ground.

"Back up."

He did. "I've done everything you've asked. If you leave her alone I'll do anything you want."

"Why?"

"Because she's innocent."

Marissa snorted.

"Why did you bring her into this in the first place?"

"Because she's the type of woman I hate. Never been touched by the harsh reality of life."

"And you have?" He didn't know how much time had passed since he'd called Geo. If he kept Marissa talking the shooters might have a chance to get in position.

"My papa worked his way up from the barrios. I'm no stranger to hardship. Unlike her. She acted as if the world would end if she couldn't come up with money for her tuition. Stupid spoiled bitch. Like playing with rocks is even a real job. She has no idea what it's really like to be poor and desperate with no options." She angrily kicked at Kenna, aiming for her ribs. But with her attention focused on Drake, she missed and hit Kenna's knee.

A keening moan escaped from Kenna's prone form.

Killing rage burned inside him. "If you hated her so much, why keep up the pretense of being her friend?"

"I hadn't planned on using her again this year until I found out about Jerry and Tito Cortez double-crossing me a few months back. Stupid bastard Jerry had developed a soft spot for her. I should've known Jerry paid her to deliver some bullshit packages to throw suspicion from Tito so his cousin wouldn't get freaked out and rat him out to the Compadres."

In his own way, Jerry Travis had protected Kenna. By keeping in contact with her via email, paying her as a courier, and setting up the meeting at the Broken Arrow, he'd intended to warn her about Marissa.

She restlessly shifted her grip on the gun. "I knew she'd make the perfect bait. I'd planned on letting Tito play with her a bit before I killed her." Marissa scowled. "But then you showed up. Another man wanting to protect her.

"I even shot at her, trying to scare her away from you so she'd come crying to me. When that didn't work I paid a guy to mug her so I could drug her and hook Cortez."

This woman was absolutely fucking psycho.

Marissa shrugged. "Worked out in the end. Actually, it's working out better than I'd hoped. With Tito dead, Kenna dead, and you dead, there's no one left alive who can connect me to Diablo. There'll be chaos among the big boys and I'll take my place at my father's table, as I should have long ago. Then he can't ignore me."

"Who's your father?"

"Hector Valero."

Shit. Marissa's father was Jerry Travis's boss. Valero had handed over the reins to his son, her brother, Alejandro, five years ago. Alejandro now ran the entire north side of Miami. Evidently they'd never thought to include Marissa in the family business. Didn't matter. She'd definitely developed their taste for blood and power.

"Clever, getting me to talk about my father. But the information won't help you."

She leveled the gun at him and Drake knew this was it.

A glaring beam of light shone in Marissa's eyes, effectively blinding her.

"Drug Enforcement!" Geo's amplified voice reverberated through the room, yet there was no sign of him. "Drop the gun. Now!"

"No!" Marissa screamed and swung the gun, firing wildly.

Drake dove for the floor and covered his head.

Several shots rang out. He heard, rather than saw Marissa's body crumple to the ground.

Geo shouted, "Clear!"

A flurry of activity filled the room. Everything faded into the background as Drake focused on the only thing that mattered: Kenna.

He crawled to her. The concrete floor scraped the skin from his bare knees. When he reached her, his stomach clenched.

Bruises dotted her hairline. Blood trickled from her nose. Her skin was ghostly pale. Drake did a quick pat down of her limbs and torso, checking for gunshot wounds. None. He gently placed his fingertips on her carotid artery and his own pulse leapt when her heartbeat throbbed beneath his thumb.

"Hang on, hot stuff, I'm here. You're gonna be fine." He needed to free her from the damn chair. He'd tear through the tape with his teeth if he had to. Then he remembered the knife Marissa had dropped and he crawled toward it. His arm shook. Through sheer determination he steadied his hand as he held the knife.

While he sliced through the duct tape binding her hands and legs, he babbled. Words of endearment. Promises. Threats. Anything he could think of to take his mind off the fact the woman he loved was lying on a grimy floor bleeding and unconscious.

Finally the bonds were free.

Drake carefully scooped her into his arms. Her head lolled on his shoulder. She flopped, limp as a rag doll. When she didn't stir, he stared at her helplessly for what seemed like hours.

Please baby, be okay. Please baby, wake up.

"Boss?" Bobby said.

He didn't lift his eyes from Kenna's face. "What?"

"Sir, you shouldn't have moved her. You've got to let her go. The EMTs are here. They'll take care of her now."

A gurney appeared. He set her down, his arms empty. With just a fingertip, he brushed a bloody tendril of hair from her cheek. Before he lost the chance he pressed his lips to hers.

God. Hers were so cold.

Drake didn't know what to say. Seemed unfair to tell her he loved her when she couldn't respond. All he could do was wait and hope like hell he'd have a second chance.

••

Kenna drifted in and out. During one cognitive moment she couldn't help but focus on the loud voices she heard arguing in the hallway outside her hospital room.

"You go in there and wake her up to ask some stupid questions and I'll throw your ass down the stairs."

"Gonna have to grow a little bit, princess."

A laugh followed. A melodious laugh she recognized immediately. Shawnee.

But who in the world was Shawnee yelling at?

"You think it's funny? Threatening to inflict bodily harm on a federal agent?"

Was that Geo? Drake's partner? The mild-mannered, soft-spoken Geo? Shouting back at Shawnee?

Maybe it was the drugs. She had to be dreaming. She closed her eyes but the argument escalated.

"What? Don't they issue you G-men a sense of humor when you get your billy club and badge, Field Agent Costas?"

"If your jokes were half as funny as your ridiculous posturing, I'd be laughing my ass off, Ms. Good Shield. Now move."

"No."

"I'm warning you."

"No. I'm warning you. Back off. Now."

Shoes squeaked. Feet scuffled.

A heavy sigh. "You really gonna make me arrest you?"

"If that's what it takes for you to leave her the hell alone."

"Didn't get enough jail time the first go around?"

Kenna winced. Waited for the sound of Shawnee's hand to meet Geo's face.

But Shawnee laughed again. "Why am I not surprised you jerks ran my records? What happened to an individual's right to privacy?"

"Superseded by 9/11 and the Patriot Act."

"Did you get off on what nasty little secrets you found out about me?"

No answer.

"Come on, G-man, you don't look the least bit sorry. So am I as dangerous as my criminal profile claims?"

"You are even more dangerous than I ever imagined," Geo said softly.

Dead silence.

"W-well. Good."

Shawnee tongue-tied? What was going on?

"Can I do my job now?"

"I'll make you a deal; you can talk to her if she's awake. But if she's sleeping, you're out of there so fast your fancy loafers will be smoking."

"Fine."

Kenna turned her head toward the wall. She didn't want to talk to anyone besides Drake.

Footsteps stopped at the side of her bed.

"Satisfied? Now get out." Shawnee hissed. "Hey. Let go of me."

"If I can't talk to her, I'll just have to talk to you."

"That wasn't part of the deal."

"I know. Funny how fast things can change, isn't it, princess?"

Shawnee's scathing reply was lost as they drifted out of range and Kenna drifted off to sleep.

CHAPTER NINETEEN

One week later…

The air conditioner had conked out again. Kenna didn't care. Even in the sweltering August heat she couldn't seem to get warm. She clutched the tattered afghan and let her head droop to the back of the couch.

No matter how much she slept, she couldn't get comfortable. She couldn't forget the terror of nearly losing her life.

Everything had changed drastically. Finishing the last year of school, strangely enough the driving reason for becoming involved with Marissa in the first place, didn't seem nearly as important.

Shawnee had returned home for five days, insistent on taking care of her. As usual Shawnee hadn't gone into much detail about the family emergency involving her brother Santee, and she'd been extremely pensive about problems at the dig site. Still, Kenna had been glad to have her around, even if Shawnee spent most of the time bitching about "that Greek detective from hell."

She shoved a pillow under her neck and sighed.

The headaches from the concussion were manageable with pain medication. The skin on her arms and calves where the tape had chafed was beginning to lose some of the redness. The bruises on her face were still a grotesque mixture of yellow, gray and green. Her body was sore, but it had started to heal.

Too bad she couldn't say the same about her heart.

Kenna hadn't seen Drake since that awful afternoon. Granted, she'd been knocked out and missed the whole damn showdown. After she'd awoken in the hospital, the doctors insisted on keeping her overnight for observation and banned all visitors. She wondered how much Shawnee had to do with that edict. So she'd spent a restless night worrying about Drake and suffering through her own injuries.

Bobby had driven her home late the next morning after Geo had asked questions and taken her statement. Although Geo had been solicitous, he hadn't given her any information about Drake beyond the news he hadn't been seriously hurt.

So why hadn't Drake the super spy been around to wrap things up when he'd been so adamant about Diablo being "his" case from the very beginning?

The Diablo case was closed. Jerry was dead. Marissa was dead. So was Tito Cortez. Kenna remembered the cold look in Marissa's eyes, but everything after she'd hit the floor remained mercifully blank.

Sometimes blurred memories danced just beyond her mental grasp. The sound of Drake's soothing voice. The gentle touch of his hands. A sweet kiss. Half the time Kenna wondered if she'd dreamed it. Or maybe it was wishful thinking. Drake's concern for her hadn't extended to a phone call or even a brief visit.

Obviously she'd read more into their time together than he had. Okay. Not his fault she'd fallen head over heels in love with him, the jerk. After the intensity of their connection, she thought he'd have the balls to face her before he hightailed it back to Florida.

Love sucked. Since she'd never been in love, she'd never believed those sappy love songs wailing about how much love hurt. A sob rose in her throat and she choked it back. God. If she started bawling again she might never stop.

Three raps sounded on her door. Kenna glanced at the clock. 6:30. Suppertime. She ignored the summons, assuming it was snoopy Mrs. Mahoney. She wasn't in the mood for company or for another tuna casserole.

When the distinctive knock "shave-and-a-haircut-*pause*-two-bits" echoed, she froze.

Slowly, she lifted her head from the back of the couch and listened. There it was again. The same rhythm, a little louder.

Drake?

Her heart slammed and she nearly skipped to the door.

She didn't bother peering through the peephole; she just unlocked the door and hoped.

Drake stood on the threshold, knuckles poised to knock again, his other hand clutching a spray of lavender orchids.

Her eyes ate him up. It wasn't fair for a man to look so good. His handsome face was clean-shaven, the long-sleeved white shirt he wore was pressed, as were the khaki pants.

Their gazes met. His was unreadable, hers, she knew, wary.

"Hi," he said.

"Hi," she said.

"Is this a bad time?"

"No."

He thrust the flowers at her. "These are for you."

"Ah. Thanks. Please. Come in." She stepped aside and shut the door behind him, clasping the flowers. Was this an official visit? Or was he coming to say goodbye?

Kenna faced him with a fake half-smile, which died the minute she saw his furious look. "What?" she snapped.

"I can't believe what she did to your beautiful face." Drake reached over and traced his fingertips over the bruises.

Her breath caught at his show of tenderness.

He moved back quickly as if he'd been burned. "Are you okay?"

"Getting there."

"Good." He raked a hand though his damp hair, releasing the woodsy scent of his shampoo.

Kenna's knees buckled, remembering how thoroughly he'd lathered her breasts, her belly and every slick inch of her body with that shampoo.

He sighed and glanced around anxiously, acting like her crappy little apartment was the last place he'd wanted to be.

She couldn't stand another second of his guarded perusal. "Agent March, why are you here?"

"To see how you're doing."

"If you've come to alleviate your guilt, I'm fine, as you can plainly see." She whirled toward the curio cabinet, placing the flowers on top as she rummaged for a vase.

Drake turned her back around. "Well, I'm not fine."

"How is that my problem—" And then his mouth was on hers, hot, hungry and forceful.

Relief washed through her. Kenna wound her arms around his neck, breathed his familiar tang deep into her lungs and welcomed the warmth she hadn't felt in days.

After they were both breathless, he kissed his way up the side of her face, gently brushing his mouth over the string of bruises along her hairline. "I'm so glad you're all right. I swear my heart stopped when Marissa had that knife to your throat." He shuddered. "And afterwards, when you were just lying on the floor, not moving, I was so afraid I'd lost you."

"Yeah? Well, I thought you'd lost my address, since I haven't seen or heard from you."

Drake pulled away from her slightly and frowned. "I've been in Miami. Didn't Geo tell you?"

"No." Geo had been too busy arguing with Shawnee.

"No wonder you're so pissy," he murmured.

"I am *not* pissy."

"Yes, you are, but that's okay because that's the way I like you best." His palm swept up her arm, over her shoulder and lingered on the spot where her pulse pounded. He cupped the side of her face in his hand. "Did you miss me?"

"No."

"Liar." He smiled. "I missed you too."

He began to stroke his thumb lightly across her jawbone. A seduction. A sweet distraction. When she found herself melting against him, her back snapped straight. "So why are you here instead of in Miami?"

"Tying up some loose ends."

"Such as?"

"You aren't going to make this easy, are you?"

"Make what easy? You waltzing in here to tell me 'hey, it's been fun, but I gotta get back to my real life'?"

Just like that, he released her. "That's what you think?"

"What am I supposed to think?"

"You're not supposed to think, Kenna, you're supposed to know that after all we've been through in the last week I wouldn't just 'waltz' away from you. Jesus. What kind of man do you think I am?"

She didn't answer. Couldn't without giving too much of herself away.

His eyes narrowed until there was no trace of blue left. "Is that all I've been to you? A walk on the wild side? An adventure? A man you'd take to bed but not good enough to be seen in public with without wearing a disguise?"

Horrified by his shallow opinion of her, she gasped. "No!"

He grabbed her by the upper arms. "Then tell me goddammit. Tell me what you want from me."

Kenna didn't even hesitate. She just blurted, "Everything, all right? I want everything from you."

The tension in his face disappeared. "Thank you."

Immediately she shrank back. *That was it? Thank you? For dropping my soul at your feet? For letting you see my heart in my eyes?*

Feeling like a fool, she angled her face from view, checking for a hole in her chest where her heart used to be.

She waited for him to say something, anything, but the silence between them grew.

"Look at me," he said softly.

"I can't," she whispered.

"You have to." Very gently he tipped her chin higher. "I want to look in those gorgeous lavender eyes when I tell you I love you."

The room spun. "You d-do?"

"Yep. I was a goner from the moment you told me to fuck off." He kissed her again, sweetly, delicately, with less certainty than she was used to from him. "You drive me crazy, which is fair because I'm sure I drive you crazy too."

Kenna burst into tears.

He held her. Murmured declarations of absolute devotion. When the storm of her emotions passed, she placed a kiss on his heart and gazed into his eyes. "This happened so fast. I didn't know if it was real."

"I don't think it gets any more real than this, sweetheart."

"Even if I'm just plain, old boring Kaye?"

Confusion darkened his face. "Why are you talking about?"

"Kenna isn't real, Drake. She's flamboyant, outrageous, argumentative. She does things I'd never do." She bit her lip and blurted, "Kenna isn't really me."

How did Drake react to her dramatic and heart-wrenching confession?

He rolled his eyes.

"Bullshit," he said. "Maybe in the past you've hidden that part of you, for whatever reason, but it's always been there. And I'm not talking about the sexy clothes and all that junk. Or what name you call yourself or even the name I call you. That isn't what defines a person." He tapped her heart, then her temple. "This does."

Omigod. He really did love her. She started to cry again.

"Those had better be happy tears," he groused.

"They are." She settled her cheek against his chest and listened to his heart beating. Strong. Steady.

About thirty seconds passed before he demanded, "Well? Don't you have something to say to me?"

"Impatient much?"

"Come on. I'm dying here, Kenna."

She circled her arms around his neck. "I love you."

"Yeah?" His beaming grin was a sight to behold. "Do tell."

"The last week has been pure hell. I missed you so much it seemed like part of me was gone. I was so confused because I didn't know how you felt."

"Every time I made love to you I showed you exactly how I felt." Drake hooked his arms under her butt and lifted her until her legs wrapped around his hips. Kissing her, he walked them backward until her spine hit the door. "In fact, I'd better show you again right now so you don't forget."

The brush of his body against hers turned her blood into liquid fire. Need, desire, love, ran rampant through her system. Drake buried his lips in her throat. He ground his cock into the soft notch between her thighs. His heat swamped her until she surrendered to the passion, arched and cried out.

He stopped and gave her a guilty look. "Oh man, I didn't think about you still being hurt. Are you feeling up to this?"

"Yes." Kenna licked his lower lip, then yanked his mouth back where it belonged.

Drake growled and shoved her cotton gym shorts to the side, so he could touch her where she was warm and wet for him. He pulled back and grinned. "No panties. I like that naughty side of you."

Bracing her against the door with his upper body, he dropped his pants and boxers to his knees. He paused, keeping the smooth, hot head of his cock poised at her entrance.

"I love you," he said, and slowly slipped inside her.

They moaned at the same time.

Fast and furious, no time for whispered endearments, just an intense show of need. Kenna felt the familiar tightening in her lower belly as Drake let loose a deep groan. The door rattled as he hammered into her. When she reached the point of no return, he tipped them both over the edge and swallowed her cries of pleasure.

Breathing hard and still seated inside her, his damp forehead sagged to her shoulder. "Shit."

"What?"

"No condom."

"Umm. I think I'm safe." Probably. Maybe.

"We'll be married anyway if you get pregnant, so it won't matter."

Kenna grabbed his hair in her fists, and forced him to look her in the eye. "Married? Kids? Aren't you jumping the gun? We haven't even talked about the fact your job is in Florida—"

"As of yesterday, I don't work in Florida." When she gave him a blank stare, he playfully nipped her chin. "Ask me why I went to Miami right away and let Geo wrap up my case."

"Why did you go to Miami?"

"I handed in my request for a transfer."

She blinked. Was he serious? Her heart sped up again.

"I figured with you almost being done with school, it'd be easier for me to move here. Plus, I was getting burned out working with the dregs of society day in and day out. The local office is happy to have me, even if I won't be in the field full-time. I'll be another nine-to-five suit and tie guy."

"I thought you loved being secret agent spy man."

"I do. But I love you more."

Tears prickled her eyes.

"Ah shit. Don't cry."

"I can't help it. That's the most romantic thing I've ever heard."

"Real romantic," he snorted. "I just banged you against the door, my pants are still around my ankles—"

230 | LORELEI JAMES

"Do I seem upset?"

Drake's face softened with the look she was beginning to recognize as love. "No. It humbles me that you accept my harsher edges. Hell, you seem to prefer them. You know I'm bossy. I'm used to being in charge and I like it that way. But I swear I'll do everything I can to make you happy. I'm not the most sophisticated man, but I do have a college degree and I'll try like hell not to embarrass you in front of your colleagues, Doc."

Kenna slapped his naked flank. "Don't be an ass. I don't give a crap what anyone thinks about you or about us. Besides, I'll have to sit this semester out anyway."

Drake shifted his hips and slipped from her body. He gently set her feet on the floor and stepped back to yank up his clothes.

"No, you won't."

Her gaze sharpened as she adjusted her own clothing. And was it her imagination or was Drake taking an incredibly long time to fasten his pants? "What are you talking about?"

He scooted back. Way back. "Don't get mad. I talked to the registrar this afternoon and I, umm…I paid your tuition."

"What!"

"You can think of it as a wedding gift. Trust me, I'm getting the better end of the deal. Before too long you'll be supporting me. Federal agents are notoriously underpaid." He grinned.

The indignation she expected to feel never came. It appeared this gorgeous, sweet, gruff man would go to any lengths to ensure her happiness. How had she gotten so lucky? "Thank you."

Drake seemed surprised she hadn't argued. "You are going to marry me, aren't you?"

She crossed her arms over her chest. "I don't recall you asking."

That uncertain expression flitted across his handsome face again. "See? I suck at this stuff." He sighed. "I wanted this moment to be romantic. I brought you flowers, I wanted to ask you to marry me on bended knee, but the truth is my damn knees are pretty scabbed over from crawling across the concrete."

"When did you do that?"

"After Marissa went down. I didn't notice until later because I couldn't think beyond anything but getting to you."

Kenna knew they'd both have nightmares of that awful afternoon. Time would dim the horrors and love would carry them through whatever else lay ahead. "So, where's the ring?"

"I haven't bought you a ring."

"You really do suck at this."

"Yet," he added. "But I did bring the motorcycle. Wanna go for a spin?"

She grinned. "Absolutely. I'll grab some condoms."

As they drove off into the fading purple sunset, Kenna knew her life with the devilish Drake March would be one wild ride.

ABOUT THE AUTHOR

Lorelei James is the *New York Times* and *USA Today* best-selling author of contemporary erotic romances. Her books have been nominated for and won the Romantic Times Reviewer's Choice Award as well as the CAPA Award. Lorelei also writes gritty, award winning mysteries set in the worlds of bikers and ranchers, under the name **Lori Armstrong.** She lives in western South Dakota.

Want to connect with Lorelei? Here's how:

Pop over to Facebook
www.facebook.com/LoreleiJamesAuthor

Follow Lorelei James on Twitter at
www.twitter.com/loreleijames

Stop by the Lorelei James website
www.LoreleiJames.com

Sign up for my Lorelei James newsletter
www.LoreleiJames.com/newsletter.php

Made in the USA
San Bernardino, CA
04 February 2015